EBOLA '76

Amir Tag Elsir was born in the north of Sudan in 1960. He has published ten novels, two biographies and various collections of poetry, with work translated into several languages. His novel *The Grub Hunter* was short-listed for the 2011 International Prize for Arabic Fiction (IPAF) and published in English translation in 2012; another novel, *366*, was long-listed for the same prize in 2014.

AMIR TAG ELSIR

EBOLA '76

Translated by
Charis Bredin and Emily Danby

DARF PUBLISHERS
LONDON

Published by Darf Publishers 2015

Darf Publishers LTD, 277 West End Lane, London, NW6 1QS

Copyright © Amir Tag Elsir 2012
First published in Arabic as *ebola76* by Saqi Books, Beirut in 2012
English Translation Copyright © Charis Bredin & Emily Danby 2015

Cover by Luke Pajak

www.darfpublishers.co.uk

Twitter: @darfpublishers
ISBN 9781850772743
eBook ISBN 9781850772811

Printed and bound in Turkey by Mega Printing

Typeset by Palimpsest Book Production Limited, Falkirk, Stirlingshire

In times of tragedy
All appears real
Eyes are real
The hand that greets a neighbour is real
The moon is no longer a distant fantasy
It is real
My lover questions me about the meaning of reality
I refer her to tragedy
Passers-by ask me, 'What is real blood?'
And I say, 'Real blood is that which tragedy spills'

In August 1976, the deadly Ebola virus struck numerous regions of the Democratic Republic of the Congo (or Zaire, as it was called at the time) and the border region of Nzara in the south of Sudan. The virus, causing fatal haemorrhagic fevers, is believed to have been carried across the border by a textile factory worker. This is neither the story of that factory worker nor any other character that appears in the course of the narrative. It is a work of pure fiction, bearing no relation to reality. All references to the rebellion and civil war are also fictitious, and unfounded in historical events.

ONE

It was a blazing afternoon in August 1976, and the deadly Ebola had begun its pursuit of Lewis Nawa, fiercely determined to infiltrate his bloodstream.

Lewis was from the borderlands of Nzara in the south of Sudan, a blue-collar worker in a small factory producing cotton garments. The factory was owned by a certain James Riyyak, a former dissident in the rebel army that had long been revolting against the central authorities in Khartoum. Lewis had gone to Congo to mourn his lover, having learnt of her death from a traveller recently returned from Kinshasa. For two years now the woman in question had occupied his every thought and desire, monopolising all of the affection he had previously reserved for his wife. Having arrived in the centre of Kinshasa, Lewis remained just long enough to glance cautiously from left to right, before hurrying across the unpaved road to a minibus which would take him to a small cemetery on the outskirts of the city. There, Ebola's many victims lay side by side, struck down in the overwhelming chaos of its recent outbreak.

The cemetery was enclosed by a white stone wall and a border of trees, some in leaf and others already with their branches bare. As Lewis entered, Ebola was all around. It hovered inches from him, anticipating its moment to pounce. The virus had already claimed the bodies of most of the people he encountered there. It coursed through the blood of the old, sunken-cheeked beggar woman as she silently extended her hand towards Lewis to receive his half franc. It had infiltrated the veins of the stern guard, who now leant against his battered old rifle, his gaze flitting between the visitors as they came and went through the main gates. It inhabited the many mourners who passed before Lewis's distracted gaze. Even as he knelt in tears beside the grave of his lover, who had died just two days previously, the virus was there, lurking in her corpse beneath the soil.

The deadly Ebola was not entirely sure what it found so intriguing about Lewis Nawa, but something about him had propelled it into a fit of excited agitation, and it had resolved to enter his bloodstream and migrate to another land. The virus had been terrorising its home country for some time now and everywhere a refrain of mournful wailing rang out, while the authorities had mobilised every force of good and evil to hunt down the killer and uncover its identity. Samples of blood from its many victims had reached the laboratories of wealthy western countries. In America, Canada and Australia, scientists were hunched over sophisticated microscopes, searching for a vaccine or cure to consign the virus to oblivion.

To be frank, Lewis was not particularly physically alluring. He certainly was not handsome, with a bulbous nose peppered with stubborn white pimples, and shoulders that were a little too broad. His lips were always dry and cracked, due to the heat and his constant state of dehydration, while the centre of his wide forehead was branded with the sacred and rather ugly markings that distinguished his tribe.

How old Lewis was nobody knew for sure, but he looked to be in his late forties or early fifties. Up until then, his medical history had been impeccable. He had suffered neither hypertension nor diabetes, his eyesight was perfect, and his prostate and kidneys were in good order. He was afflicted only by the occasional bout of Swamp Fever, which was barely even considered an illness in those parts. In contrast, Lewis's romantic history was rather pathetic. He had made his first attempts at romance at an early age, pursuing sixteen girls in total: some his own age, as well as others both older and younger. Only one of these girls had responded to his attentions, and she also happened to be partially-sighted. Yet it had not been long before she too had abandoned him, giving no reason for her sudden flight.

It was now seven years since Lewis had finally married a woman named Tina Azacouri. Tina was from another tribe, but now lived with him in his home town of Nzara, where she sold water on the streets with her mother. During the course of her career she had been the victim of six rapes and two attempted rapes. Yet this was not the cause of her and Lewis's estrangement – that had begun only two years previously when Lewis first met the woman for whom he now wept so bitterly.

Lewis's mistress was named Elaine, although he liked to call her Elaina – not that it mattered now that the deadly Ebola had erased her forever from his life. Lewis failed to comprehend why she had been taken, along with the many others who lay beside her, mourned by their own loved ones who would soon share this same fate. Blithely unaware of this, the people of Congo continued to scoff at the warnings issued by the health authorities, and the government's attempts to alert them to a danger no one fully understood. The people were convinced that the endless parade of death marching through the villages was the work of a vengeful, wicked sorcerer, who − in reality − existed only in their impoverished imaginations.

Lewis had first met Elaine on holiday, in a shabby little hostel on the outskirts of Kinshasa. Elaine was a chambermaid with no great aspirations. Lewis began to visit her once or twice a month, bringing with him the wild lust of one newly in love and enough good food to keep them going through two days of particularly ravenous and debauched love-making. Once the two days were up, he would return to Nzara, burying himself in work and concealing his mad longing for another encounter even more frenzied and passionate than the last. Luckily for him he was absent the day the deadly Ebola entered Elaine, ravaging her body until her last drop of blood was spent. Elaine had never been faithful to Lewis, and had contracted the virus from a man who would visit her during his absence.

And now it was Lewis who had been chosen to carry Ebola back to his home country, where it would wreak more damage than ever before. As he stemmed the flow of his tears and mopped his eyes with a corner of his embroidered *thawb*, a scrawny, barefoot flower-seller approached him. The girl often travelled the short distance from her small village to the cemetery, to sell tokens of mourning to the grievers. Despite her total nonchalance towards the virus, she had not yet been infected, and held out a pansy to Lewis, its black face surrounded by a fringe of purple petals. Lewis jumped to his feet as though scalded and took three, burying them in the tear-soaked soil. As he left the cemetery his eyes continued to drift unwittingly back to the grave of his dear departed Elaine.

After passing through the main gates, Lewis immediately found himself surrounded by a crowd of men of various ages and physiognomies, all attempting to strike up a conversation with him. He could not tell whether they were acquaintances or simply fellow mourners wishing to share a particular insight. What united them all, however, was the virus lurking in their blood, ready to strike them down, one by one.

Luckily, Lewis was protected by a cotton scarf he had taken home from the factory one day. He normally wrapped the scarf around his shoulders, but on this occasion he had used it to cover the lower half of his face, in an attempt to conceal the signs of his bitter grief. Thus, he had unwittingly foiled Ebola's first assault on him, as it danced towards him suspended in the droplets of spit flying from the men's mouths as they spoke.

On his way to the main road to catch a lift back to the city centre, Lewis was next confronted by Ruwadi Monti, a famous blind guitar player known to fans and critics alike as 'the Needle.' Like Lewis, Ruwadi also belonged to the group of individuals whom Ebola had thus far failed to ensnare. In all aspects of life, he was an avid and ambitious man. He was handsome, in spite of his blank, roving eyes, and his keen senses allowed him to pick up all manner of human odour for many metres around. Ruwadi was also highly influenced by Western culture and claimed to have been educated at Brussels University, gaining the honour

of becoming the first and last blind African graduate. Such
a claim was, however, wholly unfounded – and the whole
of Kinshasa, where the Needle had lived for sixty years,
knew it to be so. Ruwadi's musical credentials were purely
African and he had obtained them with minimal effort,
from the comfort of his own home. He had once visited
Brussels, however, strumming his guitar in the Galeries
Royales, the city's busiest and most prestigious thoroughfare,
and performing in a spirited concert at the grand Théâtre
de la Monnaie, held in support of the Third World and its
many afflictions.

Ruwadi approached Lewis followed closely by Darina,
a pretty girl in her early twenties who acted as the musician's personal walking stick. Ruwadi did not want anything
in particular from Lewis. A melancholy citizen from Nzara
hardly presented fertile ground for the ego of a renowned
old musician like the Needle. From an early age, however,
Ruwadi had developed the habit of accosting people in
the street. Sometimes he did so for no reason whatsoever
and at other times – especially after he had become famous
– in order to gauge the public's opinion of him. He would
accost anyone and everyone: his own mother as she left
the house, armed men he knew to be dangerous, or even
his own shadow if he encountered it on the street. That
day Ruwadi had no particular aim, and had simply come
to engage with the cemetery-goers. He had visited Nzara
on numerous occasions, and other places both near and far.
With his trademark flamboyance, he had entertained wild
concerts packed with rapturous youths and pretty women
whose physical charms were, for obvious reasons, lost on
him. He had also experienced his fair share of failures:
audiences composed solely of the organisers and a few

diehard partygoers who refused to miss even the most lacklustre show. On several occasions Ruwadi had also been permitted to grace the tables of tribal chieftains and government ministers, along with various other important men made rich through war, and entertain them for a small fee.

Ruwadi extended a slender hand, whose great exploits deserved more accolades than they would ever receive, and ran his fingers across Lewis's forehead, identifying his tribal branding as easily as he had picked up the scent of his ragged breath. Then he snatched up a corner of his scarf and began examining it.

'Forgive me for interrupting you so abruptly and at such a moment, but the colour of your scarf has captivated me. Blue is my favourite colour.'

By pure coincidence – or perhaps it was no coincidence at all – Lewis's scarf did indeed happen to be blue, as was Ruwadi's own stylish suit and silk shirt.

'Thank you,' Lewis replied, pulling the scarf tighter around his neck and covering as large a portion of his face as possible, in an attempt to conceal the tear marks which were still plainly evident.

As he began to walk away, Lewis heard the guitar player call out behind him.

'I'm performing soon in the south of Sudan. In Nzara – your town! It will certainly be an entertaining affair . . . Come along, my sad friend. Allow yourself a little frivolity and abandon your sorrows.'

Lewis should really have been a little more taken aback by this conversation, at least by the comments about the colour of his scarf, since it was feasible the thin scars on his forehead were what had betrayed his tribe and country. Yet he showed no signs of surprise, perhaps because the sadness pulsing through his veins had temporarily obstructed such an emotion, or even obliterated it altogether. The blind guitarist's words, however extraordinary they may have been, sounded to Lewis like any other mundane remark – no different to the daily banter he exchanged at the factory with his less than remarkable colleagues, or the marketplace chitchat with the butcher, the greengrocer and the Arab traders, or the gossip of his barber, Manko Nokosho, who shaved the heads of a good third of Nzara's men, without ever begrudging his endless toil. As Lewis replayed the words in his mind, they eventually merged into his wife Tina's nagging, an endless refrain that had begun at the time of his first infidelity. At this, Lewis's thoughts settled back on Elaine. So sudden and painful was the memory that he almost returned to her grave to continue weeping and plant another bunch of pansies in the damp soil.

With complete conviction, the crowd of men at the cemetery gates informed Lewis that the death and disease ravaging the villages and towns of Congo were the work of a wicked sorcerer waging some mysterious vendetta. Lewis unquestioningly accepted their words, conditioned to do so by his upbringing and intellectual capacity. The people had certainly heard tell of a mysterious virus, and those with a decent level of education had read out to others the warnings from the Ministry of Health, poorly printed on cheap paper. The radio was another source of information, now that the traditional and uplifting melodies of Draydo Lenoah, Suleiman Agho, Ali Farka Touré and Menelik Wossenachew were regularly interrupted by news bulletins about the virus. Despite this, the wicked sorcerer remained uppermost in people's minds. Many tribes had even mobilised their own cohorts of wizened sorcerers, equipping them with materials for fashioning amulets and ordering them to hunt out evil in whatever nook or cranny it might be lurking.

Lewis hailed from a similar background to the crowd of men. His brain, like theirs, was trained to accept the simplest explanation, just as his body was composed of the same hormones and afflicted by all the same grievances: hands that remained sweaty no matter the temperature or humidity, and hair that took years to go white. And so, besides his grief for Elaine, the only new addition to Lewis's repertoire of emotions was a latent wrath against the vicious sorcerer who had killed his lover and left him in despair.

Lewis hitched a ride back to Kinshasa in an open-topped cattle truck. The driver, who looked about thirty, stopped willingly, winking at him as he climbed on board. Another man and a woman were already occupying the back in stony silence, interrupted every now and then by the man's violent cough – luckily just a symptom of a mild dose of flu. The woman sat in front of Lewis on an iron bench, and seemed to be in agonising pain as she nursed her swollen belly. Still in a daze, Lewis failed to deduce that she was in her final month of pregnancy and suffering her first contractions as her husband took her to the nearest hospital in Kinshasa. Vaguely, he assumed she must have eaten her way into such a state and was suffering the ill effects of her own gluttony.

He was lost in thought, his head lolling onto his shoulder, blind to the pleasant greenery that fringed the road and stretched into the distance as far as the eye could see. Even the stench of dung from the cattle tied up next to him barely made an impression. Thus, the woman's piercing scream came as rather a shock. As Lewis watched blood and water pooling beneath her, all he could think was that he had lived with two different women in two different countries and neither had given him a child. Before he could reflect any further on this, however, Lewis found himself dumped unceremoniously onto the road into Kinshasa. The driver had expelled him from the vehicle, winking again as he did so, before lugging the woman off to a suitable spot for delivering the child. Lewis did not give the wink much thought. Even if he had, he would never have guessed that it did not in fact result from the driver's roguish character, but from a chronic – and at that time incurable – illness affecting the nerves in his eye.

Some time later, Lewis arrived in the centre of Kinshasa, with Ebola still hot on his trail. After leaving the cattle truck, he plodded along a tedious stretch of road before being picked up by a one-eyed Congolese lorry driver. He finally disembarked in one of the capital's most respectable streets, where there were none of Ebola's usual types of prey: local eccentrics, coy prostitutes, obstinate beggars and pro-democracy protesters. The street, in fact, belonged to an old magician by the name of Jamadi Ahmed. He did not really own it, of course, but his consistent daily presence there, year in and year out, as well as his dazzling tricks, had inspired one of the street cleaners to remove the sign bearing the name Zumbi Street and replace it with another scrawl declaring it to be Jamadi Ahmed Street.

The magician was already there when Lewis arrived. His audience was not exactly what one would expect of such a distinguished magician, since his glory had been waning for many years now. Over the past decade he had lost many of the prestigious fans every true magician deserves. The entire national football team had left for more appealing lands, and several overly ambitious politicians had been executed in the streets without trial. Thanks to a string of military coups in a neighbouring country, Jamadi also risked losing the patronage of a close female relative of the country's president who came to watch him several times a year and always paid him handsomely.

Lewis joined the crowd in front of the magician and was soon enraptured by his performance. Despite having visited Kinshasa several times before, he'd never encountered the magician. He watched as Jamadi popped a fluttering dove into his canvas bag before pulling a wild rabbit out of a hole in the side. Having deposited the rabbit back in the sack, he then extracted an extremely fluffy white chicken.

Lewis applauded self-consciously, hearing only the sound of his own hands. The rest of the crowd had long since abandoned the custom of clapping, agreeing that, no matter how awkward the silence became, they would applaud only if the magician came up with some new tricks – but he had thus far failed to do so. Jamadi, meanwhile, pulled six jagged razors from the felt cap on his head and swallowed them with a groan before washing them down with a strip of red ribbon. Lewis watched in tense silence, his hands trembling as he fished a whole franc from his pocket and tossed it into the magician's almost empty cup. When Jamadi brought his hand to his mouth and pulled out the ribbon, neatly entwined with the razors, Lewis was unable to contain his amazement, laughing and rushing to embrace the magician. He had momentarily forgotten his lover was dead, a deadly killer was on the loose, and embracing a homeless magician, who fed himself on God knows what, was a risky activity best avoided.

No one could tell why the old magician rejected Lewis's impetuous gesture with such animosity, stamping his foot angrily on the ground and cutting the show off early, even though it was scheduled to continue until midnight. Jamadi started gathering his equipment and arranging it into his case as the audience muttered possible explanations to one another. Perhaps Jamadi had eaten a suspect stew at the filthy restaurant where he had dined before the show. Perhaps he had some irrational hatred of foreigners. Or perhaps Lewis's unexpected embrace had ruined a new trick he was planning to spring on an audience always eager for something new. To Ebola, however, it made no difference whether the magician laughed or cried as it continued to stalk Lewis, longing to accompany him to a new land. It only hoped that after the show's abrupt end the exhausted Lewis would move on and encounter another of its victims. At that moment, the virus was growing seriously concerned that Lewis might suddenly cut short his travels and board a bus home. If he escaped, the hunt for a victim would have to begin all over again.

Lewis stood in stunned silence before the magician's unexpected wrath, gazing questioningly at him with eyes that had begun to fill with sorrow once again. Jamadi both noted and understood this beseeching gaze, and yet chose to ignore it. He spoke to Lewis in French, gesticulating towards his box of tricks.

'Next time, kindly read this notice before launching yourself at me.'

Before joining the textile factory, Lewis had worked in the service of a French family long resident in Nzara, and so he understood the magician's words. Along with the rest of the audience, his gaze moved to the box.

'Ladies and Gentlemen!' the sign declared in bold red letters, 'You are kindly requested to refrain from shaking the performer's hand or directly embracing him, whatever the extent of your admiration.'

This sign had in fact been stapled to the case for as long as the magician himself had been around. But no one had ever read it, and over the years there had never been an outburst violent enough to draw attention to it. Yet as soon as the audience had read the sign, it was inevitable the words would become legend, spreading through the city like wildfire and entering into everyday parlance. 'My dear wife,' a husband would write on his pyjamas, 'you are kindly requested to refrain from embracing me, whatever the extent of your lust.' 'My distinguished professors,' a wheedling student would scribble on his exam paper, 'you are kindly requested to refrain from failing me, whatever the extent of my stupidity.' Perhaps the magician's sign would even inspire some new, repressive decrees: 'By order of the government,' a local newspaper would proclaim, 'the people are kindly requested to refrain from protesting, whatever the extent of their suffering.' It was a dangerous statement, concluded a journalist who happened to be present, as well as a campaigner for the rights of women and children. Having just left prison, a rebel fighter seeking some light entertainment vowed that he too would accept neither handshake nor embrace until he had completed his unfinished business. He immediately began to curse the government again, before promptly being thrown back into prison. Lewis, however, merely blinked in confusion, while Ebola squirmed anxiously. The chase continued as the man from Nzara slipped through its grasp once more.

The respectability of Jamadi Ahmed Street was entirely dependent upon the continued presence of the magician, and over the years this presence had proved reliable. The audience's faces thus filled with consternation as the old man suddenly flagged down a donkey cart and loaded his tricks on board. In went the familiar everyday tools, and the dusty old ones, entangled with spiders' webs – Jamadi was off to who knew where. The incredulous bystanders froze, certain this must be the new trick they'd been anticipating for so long. They gazed around, inspecting puddles of water, peering into battered windows, and digging their hands searchingly into their pockets. They didn't know exactly what they were looking for, but were certain all would soon become clear.

During those few tense seconds, a young girl named Kanini managed to wrench herself out of the general state of bewilderment. Kanini had been born in a stable on the outskirts of Kinshasa, to an unknown father. She had stayed there until she was eighteen, suffering constant harassment from the farm owners, their horse trainers and field labourers. Scanning the fifty or so baffled spectators, her gaze settled on Lewis. He seemed to be the least muddled of the lot and had greatly assisted her by compelling the long established magician to quit the street, thus paving the way for a new era of sin and depravity. Kanini read the sign with difficulty, her skills lying more in the physical language of lust than the rules of grammar. Hers was a purely spoken dialect, embellished with a few dirty phrases to boost business. Having left the countryside a year ago, Kanini now roamed Kinshasa in search of tourists she would accompany wherever they wished to go, whether to a fancy hotel or – more often – a dirt-cheap hostel.

Kanini was not impressed by Lewis's looks or by his physique – both were decidedly below average. Nor did he strike her as having untold wealth buried in his pockets. Yet he was the only foreigner available and, no matter how thoroughly you rinsed them, foreigners always seemed to have a little extra set aside for travel expenses and emergencies.

Hovering nearby, Ebola broke into a grin as Kanini sidled seductively up and pressed herself against Lewis. It watched as she brought her lips close to his scarred face, cackling with glee as Lewis left with the young girl whose blood it had infected the previous day. Ebola sidled after them as they stumbled through filthy, deserted alleyways until finally reaching their destination, a low building whose walls reverberated with shrieks of raucous laughter. Every now and then, drunks would totter out, barely able to remain upright.

And so the deal was sealed. Having visited Kinshasa to mourn his mistress, Lewis Nawa of Nzara was to transport Ebola to new territories.

TWO

Just four days before travelling to Kinshasa, Lewis had been awarded the title of Nzara's very own Man of the Year. The competition was not endorsed by either national or local government, and there was no medal or official certificate for the winner to hang on his wall. Nor was it a popular event, with crowds of cheering people. Such an award had simply never existed in Nzara. At Lewis's factory, however, a group of workers had taken to nominating one another for the prize every year and organising a modest celebration for the winner. In large part this was a response to International Women's Day, which turned the local females into vengeful demons who spurned their household chores, refused to feed their babies and forsook the marital bed. During the celebrations the women would flood the streets, bearing placards aloft and distributing pamphlets to every house in the town, often written in regional tribal languages. And so, in response, the factory workers had put each other's names on a list of nominees so long that the years to come would never accommodate it.

On the day of the award ceremony, Lewis had been advised to arrive in his very best suit. He was ordered to bathe, put on some aftershave and let Manko Nokosho trim his wiry hair. He was also instructed to refrain from the usual blazing rows he had with Tina, since it was important for his voice to ring out loud and clear during his acceptance speech and any musical number he might wish to perform afterwards. Lewis's colleagues also strictly forbade him from squabbling with Tina during the party itself, no matter what the provocation. They were all too familiar with the couple's daily battles over household expenditure and extramarital affairs.

It was Anami Okiyano who had first come up with the idea of a Man of the Year award. Anami was originally Kenyan, but he had been living in Nzara for longer than he could remember. Now in his sixties, he was still unmarried, and yet he had no intention of ever tying the knot. Anami organised the award ceremony every year, putting together a panel of judges made up of retired factory workers from various plants and a selection of elderly women with no obvious connection to anything. The decision-making process was then dictated by his own extremely erratic sense of judgement which – despite his otherwise impressive credentials – had long prevented him from becoming factory foreman. Naming himself Man of the Year in the first ever contest five years ago, for example, was a luxury he should perhaps not have permitted himself, but the thought had not even occurred to him.

This year the ceremony was to be quite different to previous ones. Lewis had insisted rather vociferously that he should receive his award in one of the town's public squares rather than the dusty corner of the factory James Riyyak usually permitted them to use, despite refusing to participate in the festivities himself. Lewis had further insisted that the local mayor attend the ceremony in person, despite the fact there was no actual mayor at the time, only a local army general with an overblown title who was in charge of municipal bureaucracy.

On the day itself Lewis was not as smartly turned out as he should have been. This was mainly due to the lack of beauty products in his house, and the tempestuous atmosphere that prevailed there, preventing any semblance of calm. He was wearing the brown trousers and green leaf-print shirt he wore on an almost daily basis, along with the blue cotton scarf that he was constantly twisting and tugging around his neck. Even his visit to Manko Nokosho had not succeeded, although the barber had experimented with several additional techniques, scraping a large amount of dirt and pimples from his face with a special threading treatment and using a steel comb to part Lewis's hair neatly down the middle. These services, he had announced, came at no extra cost; an exceptional favour for the man of the moment. The party was held in a public square where dissident rebels had once gathered to gossip and bury their wartime woes or to practice their rallying speeches calling for the partition of north and south. Anami introduced Lewis and called him forward to say a few words and thank all those involved in making him the winner. Yet Lewis was unable to formulate a single word. The most he could manage was a few nervous grunts, his eyes darting from left to right before he retreated into the crowd. In spite of this, the audience still saw fit to applaud him warmly.

During the following celebrations Lewis found himself, quite unusually, the centre of attention. He received a great many dignified handshakes, from the mayor and a number of chieftains who had deigned to attend the festivities. He

also accepted a few bottles of cheap aftershave, some rat-
and cockroach-repellent and a bottle of Blue Jinn, an
exceedingly potent local wine. To top it all off he was given
a small sum of money that had been scraped together by
his colleagues. It was enough to get him to Congo sooner
than expected, to spend two sinful days in the arms of
Elaine – or Elaina, as he preferred to call her. This was to
be rendered impossible, of course, by the unthinkable news
of Elaine's death. It reached him just as he was preparing
to set off, and thus he left, weighed down by an immense
burden of sorrow, to weep over his lover's grave.

The day Ebola entered his bloodstream Lewis did not
return to Nzara as planned, despite having told both his
estranged wife and his boss, James Riyyak, that he would
do so. Caught up in the newfound delights of the street,
Lewis remained in the house in Kinshasa, which shuddered
with decadent abandon and sinful laughter. There were thus
two ghouls holding Lewis at their mercy: the first was
Kanini, whose attentions had left him spent; the second
was Ebola, which had by that point entered his bloodstream
and multiplied furiously, occupying every cell in his body.
All the while, the virus anxiously fretted that Lewis might
not return home after all, and instead fall ill in his den of
iniquity, thwarting its travel plans until a new victim could
be located.

On the third day, as a sluggish dawn broke across the
capital announcing the beginning of a hot and sticky day,
Kanini presented Lewis with a scrap of paper. On it was a
list of debts, written in the most appalling French. She
owed the greengrocer, the butcher, the wine-seller, the taxi
man and a well-known pimp who went by the name of
Leo and claimed to protect the local prostitutes as they

trawled the grim streets. He demanded a monthly wage for this supposed service, despite never having kept a single girl from harm during all his years in the profession. With great deliberation, entwining Lewis in weary seduction, Kanini explained he simply must clear her debts as soon as possible so she could fully dedicate herself to his needs. Lewis, no longer sad or teary-eyed, gazed at the paper in astonishment. He was in no position to clear even a single line of the girl's debts. His empty pockets were quite unqualified for such lavish expenditure, and his middle-aged mindset was quite averse to capricious splurges of this magnitude. Lewis asked her to give him a few minutes while he fetched the money from a friend who lived nearby. Kanini agreed, believing what he said not because of his serious demeanour, nor her conviction that she had stolen his heart, but simply because she had no other choice. Having granted him an unspecified amount of time in which to complete the task, Kanini helped Lewis to his feet and into his clothes and accompanied him to the door, before retreating into the house to wait.

Lewis boarded the bus home, having made certain his passport was safely in his pocket along with a few francs to pay off any troublesome border guards. As he did so, an image sprung into his mind of a poster he had observed in recent weeks pasted all across Nzara. The poster had announced the imminent arrival of a blind Congolese guitar player, who would be playing at a large concert in the town's football stadium. Turning to scan the bus, Lewis found Ruwadi Monti seated right behind him, muttering away to the girl who had been with him at the cemetery gates. Containing his astonishment, Lewis turned back around and stared straight ahead, only to hear the guitar player's voice addressing him directly: 'Together to Nzara, my melancholy friend and his blue scarf. What a strange coincidence!'

This time, however, the musician's keen powers of detection had failed him, since Lewis Nawa was no longer sad and had left his blue scarf at Kanini's. He had not forgotten it, nor had the girl stolen it – he had left it there of his own accord.

THREE

Upon his arrival in Nzara, Lewis and Tina enjoyed a short period of renewed intimacy. This did not come about by chance, but because after more than two years of complete emotional estrangement, Tina had resolved herself to rekindle their relationship, carrying out the most meticulous of preparations for a romantic reunion. Lewis was also eager, since the taste of Kanini and the memory of their passionate nights together had proven rather difficult to shake off, and a flood of troublesome hormones continued to rage through his body. In a moment of grave and humbling self-doubt, Lewis decided he would strive to please Tina in any way possible, knowing for a fact she would not, under any circumstances, be anticipating his return as most wives anxiously await their husbands.

Tina was thirty-seven. Although not beautiful, she was far easier on the eye than her graceless husband. Using some savings she had been squirreling away during her long years as a water-seller, she had succeeded in making herself quite presentable. Her hair was decorated with ribbons, beads and sequinned hair clips, her face was lightly moisturised and powdered, and her eyelashes had been treated to a flourish of mascara. The house had also been improved with a few feminine touches, so that, although humble, it was now perfectly homely.

In no way was Tina in love with Lewis and nor did she ever expect to be, despite the fact that, for most of the girls of Nzara, to live and to love were one and the same thing. Whether beautiful or ugly, all had dreams of the most strange and wild suitors, from the wayward rebels in the wanted posters pasted up across the town to the swift, muscular hunting dogs that darted through the forests and returned with marvellous winnings. When performing troupes came to town, the women would even fall for the voices of the puppets on stage, while the younger girls staged imaginary weddings with the sly Mr Fox, whose wily rabbit-catching antics they read about in illustrated children's books, printed in neighbouring countries rich enough to produce editions in different local languages. But no, Tina truly had no love for Lewis. She had married him confident that there were no other proposals coming her way and that it was therefore her only miserable option. She was nearly thirty at the time, and had resigned herself to a life of spinsterhood.

It was more than seven years ago now that Lewis had unexpectedly descended on her one afternoon. By all considerations he was still young, yet his youth was marred by his unpleasant physiognomy and, in particular, by the marks on his forehead, which were more pronounced back then. In spite of his height and solid frame, Lewis bore no resemblance to a great warrior. Great warriors, after all, do not approach women, even if they are madly in love with them. Nor did he appear to be a hunter, since hunters are softly spoken and light of foot, like the gazelles they bring back for supper. In short, the only person Lewis resembled was Lewis. But then, Tina reflected in bemusement, did anyone in the world resemble anyone other than themselves?

That day, she had returned from a remote well with her mother. They had placed their buckets of water in front of them and sat down on two low stools strung together from wood and rope. Every now and then, the pair would be approached by a thirsty customer – or someone who thought himself to be thirsty. For a few dirhams Tina or her mother would scoop some water into a small aluminium cup, attached to the main bucket by a long piece of string to ensure nobody made off with it. In truth, selling water on the streets was not a particularly noble profession. Indeed, there are many professions which are superior, a few equal, and a handful inferior. Despite this, both women loved their job and worked with enthusiasm. Fate alone determines your profession in life, and if Tina or her mother had been asked that age-old question, 'If you weren't a water-seller in the street, what would you be?' both would have answered the same way. 'If I weren't a water-seller in the street I'd be a . . . a water-seller in the street!'

There was only one problem with being a water-seller, and it had nothing to do with the extremes of hot and cold the women suffered working outdoors, since the local houses were also hot in summer and cold in winter. Nor was it the continuous equatorial rain, since most homes in the neighbourhood were so poorly constructed they failed to keep the water out anyway. The problem was the street itself, and the kind of lascivious and unwelcome harassment it encouraged. This was further exacerbated by that tacit agreement held by the majority of the human population, whereby most passers-by are averse to responding to even the most blatant cries for help.

Lewis Nawa stood before the two women. Having left the service of the French family that very day, he had already managed to secure employment in the textile factory, newly opened just a few weeks ago. He was not thirsty, nor did he imagine himself to be thirsty: but he had made an impulsive resolution to marry the first girl he saw who happened to be smiling. And at that moment, chance would have it that Tina had a smile on her face. She had just remembered she was wearing a pair of her mother's particularly threadbare trousers, coupled with a rather tight blouse, and the thought had brought a smile to her lips.

Very quietly, and without hesitation or a hint of irony, Lewis proposed to Tina Azacouri.

'Today, I have resolved to marry you, whatever your name and tribe. I have a small house nearby, two fair-sized cows and a new job in a factory. It is also very likely that I can give you children. Does my proposition please you?'

'It does,' Tina replied.

'Then let's be married this very hour,' concluded Lewis in the same calm tone.

That evening, Tina's family accepted Lewis's two cows, along with a handful of dirhams and a meagre assortment of trinkets hardly deserving the accolade 'dowry.' Her mother was present, accompanied by her uncle Majouk, a performer in the Nzara Folk Dance Troupe. And of course the spirit of her father was there, too. The family firmly believed he continued to float about the house, sharing in their joys and sorrows and occasionally roaming farther afield to dance at a wedding or weep at a funeral. Tina's own ceremony was a very humble affair. Uncle Majouk and a few members of his troupe performed some jigs, and then Anami Okiyano announced that he intended to perform a song. Unfortunately, he possessed a voice barely fit for wailing at a funeral and had only sung publicly once before, when crowning himself as Man of the Year.

The newlyweds lived the most ordinary of lives together. Tina didn't stop selling water on the street – even during their honeymoon – and shortly after their marriage Lewis began to pursue other women. His first affair was with Elaine, the unfussy chambermaid from the shabby hostel in Kinshasa who gave him whatever he wanted, albeit without often looking him in the eye or enquiring about his life beyond their room. Although Tina had never seen this lover in the flesh, nor imagined she ever would, she knew everything about her. She knew her name and every detail of her face. She knew her shoe size and how many morsels of food it took to fill her stomach. She knew how she greeted Tina's unfaithful husband when he visited her, laden with desire and appetising food. And she knew the way she waved him goodbye whenever he departed. She knew the colour of the sheet spread over their adulterous bed, and the scent of the perfume she wore. She even knew of her demise at the hands of the sorcerer spreading death through the villages and towns of Congo. There was no sanctity to secrets in those parts; some people were privy to them, some were adept at overhearing them, and others delivered them to the doors of local gossips. The only thing Tina was unaware of was Ebola's deadly movements. Had she known, she would never have entertained the thoughts she did as Lewis made his way home from Congo and would instead have forever remained an abandoned wife.

Elaine's death came as a small window of light in the

general grimness of Tina's marriage. She decided to seize
the opportunity to squeeze through that window and revive
their relationship. Lewis Nawa was truly a cheat – and every
wife can recognise a cheating husband, even if she doesn't
love him. Despite this, Tina decided to give her plan a try.
In a secret consultation with her neighbour, whose own
husband had been a cheat and had died in the very act of
adultery, Lewis's past, present and future were stripped down
for inspection. The neighbour attributed his behaviour to
a wretched childhood in the slums of al-Kartoon, the
poorest part of town. His mother, she claimed, used to
throw him into rubbish dumps so he could scavenge for
food, while his brothers were shameless thieves known to
steal clothes from washing lines. This was all new to Tina,
and at first she had difficulty believing it. Eventually,
however, she accepted it as fact, nodding her head in assent.
In reality, the neighbour had dreamed up the stories out
of thin air. With slight trepidation, she reminded Tina of
Lewis's advancing years, and of his appearance, which time
had not treated kindly. After questioning her on a number
of issues entirely unrelated to Lewis's infidelity, she suggested
the couple start afresh, and try for a child. By her reckoning,
it would take some time for a man of Lewis's physical
attributes to find a new mistress – and by then he might
no longer be up to the task. This theory was rather dubious
– without any scientific basis – particularly as Tina had no
idea of the current state of her husband's prowess. She
couldn't say whether it remained the same as two or three
years ago, whether it had deteriorated, or dwindled entirely
to nothing. She had also heard that advancing years can
increase a man's appeal, in spite of his other shortcomings,
and was unable to decide whether or not this was true.

Ultimately, however, her neighbour's plan appealed to her and she decided to go ahead with it.

First, Tina practised expressing some emotion, so she could appear to be overcome with passion upon Lewis's return. In the process, she managed to win over an alley cat and a stray dog. She also ended up purchasing a number of entirely useless items – pencils, a palm frond hat and some polyester hankies – from a little orphan girl who approached her in the street as she wept.

It was a long time since Tina had wept with joy, and she began practising so intensively that the slightest occurrence would set her off. Dinner at her mother's had caused her to break down completely, even though she had eaten there hundreds of times before without ever feeling the need to weep.

She simply couldn't remember how to greet a husband returning from abroad, and didn't know how to predict his reaction to seeing her. Practising a warm embrace with the beams that held up their mud brick house or the papaya trees outside seemed a futile exercise, since inanimate objects did not present nearly the same challenges as animate ones.

Having put the finishing touches to Lewis's favourite dishes, which she had not cooked in years, Tina covered their cheap wooden bed with the same red quilt she had used on their wedding night, when she was still a virgin. Then she went to the market, a place thronging with Arab perfumers from the North whose scents had filled Southern nostrils for generations. She bought a range of products promising to make the female body soft and tender, to restore its virginal touch and make the home, however miserable and poor, a place for passion and intimacy. Having finished her preparations, Tina asked her mother for a short holiday from work. She termed it 'winning-Lewis-back leave,' but, unable to ignore the possibility of Lewis rejecting her, she secretly coined a second name: 'doing-Lewis-in leave.' If he did spurn her, treating her less than respectfully, this would become the only apt description for her time off work.

Lewis did not return on the day she had expected him, nor the next. On the third day she sat and waited for him, feeling more determined than ever to smother him with affection.

Yet as Lewis travelled home his thoughts were in fact completely attuned with Tina's, although he was unaware of this. It was as though their minds were one. Tina was busy fine-tuning the arrangements for their reunion, removing several rocks she had previously placed by the front door in the hope that Lewis would trip over and crack his head. Lewis, meanwhile, was dreaming of the virginal red quilt, the arousing perfume Tina had worn so many years ago, and various other enticing memories, some of which had actually occurred and others that were pure fantasy. As the bus approached the border – far from medical checkpoints or international quarantine laws – Lewis listened absentmindedly to Ruwadi Monti's chatter. The blind guitar player was dreamily calculating the great profits he would make in his upcoming concert, refusing to entertain the possibility of failure. There was one particularly tiresome question he would not stop repeating. Lewis wished it were a mosquito so he could squash it and have some peace:

'What kind of audience can I expect from the youth of Nzara, my melancholy friend? I haven't visited your country in years!'

At first, Lewis had answered with the greatest respect, speaking about his own tastes and adamantly denying any special inclination for modern music, or any other music for that matter. Besides, he knew nothing about the younger generation, having married late in life and produced no offspring to tell him about it. His own small radio was tuned exclusively to the news, and recently he hadn't even been turning it on at all, deciding its offerings were altogether too depressing.

The guitar player fell silent, seeming convinced. In reality, however, his silence was no more than a long, sorrowful sigh, after which he launched, once again, into the same questions.

'Tell me about *any* generation, my melancholy friend – tell me about the art-lovers of your country.'

At this, Lewis headed to the back of the bus, unperturbed by the dense throng of people crowded together there. He continued the journey standing, playing out new fantasies in his mind, all involving Tina. A few minutes later, however, he was startled to see the musician had got to his feet too and – with his companion as a leaning post – had come to stand next to him, where he would remain for the rest of the journey.

'Tell me, citizen of Nzara: will my concerts sell out?'

Lewis had wanted to tell the musician his name, to prevent him calling him 'melancholy friend' or 'citizen of Nzara,' two of the most ridiculous titles he had ever heard, but he forced the thought from his mind, aware that giving Ruwadi his name would suggest he was enjoying his company, and that could not have been further from the truth.

When the bus reached the border the travellers were submitted to the usual humiliating procedures carried out by the border guards and customs officials. The men's shirts and trousers were removed and their hair examined, while inquisitive hands poked into the women's cleavages. Lewis noticed Ruwadi Monti was the only person to pass through without any hassle, while his companion was led to a small room for her breasts to be inspected. Ruwadi, however, barely seemed to notice his special treatment and, as soon as the bus rumbled off into the town, he returned to his previous line of enquiry.

Night lay darkly across the whole region of Nzara, with its scattered cities and towns casting only the faintest of glows against the inky sky. The streets of Nzara town itself seemed almost completely lifeless. Ruwadi left with the concert organisers, who had come to meet him in a small jeep. There were three of them, giddy with excitement and speaking a mixture of Congolese, Swahili and French – clearly their favoured tongue, thanks to having all spent their childhoods in Paris. The men dropped hopeful hints that the Needle might like to play a song before setting off and so Ruwadi, choking with pleasure, took his guitar from its leather case and launched into some lively music at the bus stop. Then he disappeared into the night, without accosting a single person.

Lewis did not go straight home but lingered in the almost deserted market place where he bumped into his boss Anami Okiyano, as boisterous as ever, although angered by Lewis's unexplained absence. As is the duty of any supervisor who finds his inferiors to be wanting, he gave Lewis a sharp telling-off.

'Keep thinking about what I said,' he warned him when he'd finished rebuking him, 'so that when you hear the same thing from Riyyak tomorrow morning in the factory the words will have lost their sting.' With that, Anami shook Lewis by the hand, and left. Unfortunately the two colleagues were unaware that Lewis's violent sneeze as their conversation ended had propelled a globule of Ebola-laden mucus straight into Anami's mouth, from where the happy virus was able to race on into the rest of his body. Ebola cackled wickedly as the two went their separate ways, entirely oblivious to the great joy they had brought it.

Lewis lingered for a short time in the market, and bought a string of cheap red beads, his first present for Tina in quite some time. He sat for a short while in a café, feeling nervous, before stumbling off to a well-known tavern where he bought a half bottle of strong arak and received a drunken kiss from the owner, once again failing to detect Ebola's delighted chortles. On his arrival home, Lewis noticed the rocks that had so often caused him to stub his toe were missing. Upon seeing the inside of the house he broke into a broad smile, and Ebola grinned along with him. It was filled with every delight Lewis had imagined, and others that had not even crossed his mind.

FOUR

The streets of Nzara were lined with posters announcing the blind guitar player's forthcoming concert. These had been subjected to a variety of distasteful alterations. The local children, who viewed everything as a possible source of entertainment – even their parents' underwear – had scribbled graffiti onto them, while the grown-ups preferred to tear them from the walls and replace them with pictures of naked women, dirty jokes and other lewd images. Or they would leave them where they were, but add a few amusing touches. That morning, Lewis sauntered through the streets, his jubilant mood transforming the ferocious heat into a refreshing rosy haze. The Needle's face gazed down at him from almost every corner, sporting a thick white beard, droopy ears, and large, ogling eyes in place of his sightless ones. Near the textile factory one particularly talented worker had laboured through the night over a life-size poster, replacing Ruwadi's smart blue suit with the factory's own cheaper design.

Lewis, meanwhile, had begun to feel rather unwell. The dull pain behind his eyes had extended to his whole head, his knees were stiff and his nose was running. He was also shivering slightly and one of his hands had broken out in red spots. Despite this, Lewis remained convinced that he was simply recovering from the overindulgence of the past few days, spent in the company of not only Kanini and her hungry professional's body, but then also Tina – who had rediscovered her youthful vitality after more than two years of frigidity. Lewis was truly bewildered by the power of womanly wiles. How had he been rehabilitated so effortlessly into domestic life? He had thought it impossible, but in the end even the string of red beads had proved unnecessary. At the end of the night Tina was jubilant, even when berating him for having grown so embarrassingly stout. She was happy to see him home and even wanted to try for a child, she said, to bring some new energy to their stagnant home.

Try for a child?

Lewis laughed to himself and Ebola laughed with him, having penetrated smoothly into the body of his wife, whose armoury of seductive charms had stood no chance against it. In a few days it would all be over. The authorities would be slow to act, hindered by the remoteness of the region and the superstitious beliefs of its people. By the time they caught on, the deadly killer would have finished off a third of the population without having to face any significant resistance.

While Lewis was preoccupied with thoughts of the child that had failed to materialise during his first fertile years of marriage, Ebola was celebrating the fact that there would never be a child, regardless of any lingering fecundity in the couple's reproductive organs.

Among the other decidedly secondary thoughts occupying Lewis that morning were the excuses he would have to provide to his brutish boss in order to explain his absence. It was common knowledge among the factory workers, and a quarter if not a third of the town, that despite holding a degree in Textile Science and Engineering from a Ugandan university, Riyyak had once been one of the region's most notorious rebels – before reconciling with the authorities. He had become something of a legend, and people in the town recounted numerous stories about him. Some of these – such as his faultless ability to sniff out a traitor and his astonishing skills in camouflage, which allowed him to prowl the jungles as though on a pleasant garden stroll – were true. Others were not quite as accurate – according to one, Riyyak owned a giant cobra that could easily swallow an adult whole; another claimed he drank a cup of blood every night before bed.

Despite the measly salary Riyyak paid his workers – closer to what you might hand a beggar on the street than an employee – the men clung to their jobs, never daring to question the rules for fear of the unemployment that would inevitably follow. Riyyak would remind them, often without any provocation at all, of the thousands of skilled workers in neighbouring countries awaiting his signal to leave their homes and come join him. During the seven years the factory had been in business, it had seen no unrest among its employees that honestly merited being called a strike or a mutiny. The unemployed vied for vacancies, and fathers deprived their sons of the few opportunities available for education, whisking them from the hands of European priests and earnest locals, and delivering them to James Riyyak. He would happily find them a job, apparently forgetting the sign written in his own hand hanging over the factory gates proclaiming 'No to child labour!'

Once, Riyyak had even tried to employ women for a wage vastly lower than that given to his male employees. Yet this unprecedented venture had ended in failure, since the mere presence of a woman, however butch she might be, was enough to paralyse production in that most macho of environments.

Riyyak was not on good terms with his employee Lewis Nawa. This was not entirely for personal reasons. In general, there was no love lost between the boss and his workers, whom he looked upon as hungry wretches crouching before him for a bite to eat. The workers, in turn, viewed Riyyak as a home-grown colonialist, far more ruthless than any foreign conqueror.

At six o'clock sharp on the sixth of August, 1976, Lewis finally arrived at the factory. It was fairly close to his house – but then again nowhere in that small, dusty town was very far from anywhere else, even for the elderly and the gammy-kneed. Lewis was accustomed to covering the distance at a brisk yet comfortable pace and never felt the need to go by bicycle, donkey or – as some of his lazier colleagues preferred – by piggyback service from one of the town's many unemployed. Six years ago, Riyyak had promised the workers he would provide a bus to bring them to work, something like the Indian Tata buses or Ugandan *jogojogo*. But Riyyak did not keep his word, and the promise lingered enticingly in the workmen's minds for years, with no one daring to remind him about it.

Lewis was not surprised to find his boss waiting for him. Riyyak's hulking body was tensed, like a warrior lion sung of by young girls in times gone by, its fearsome roar causing all the jungle to flee in fear. His face, meanwhile, was twisted into a hideous expression, uncannily resembling

that of the cement statue appropriately named 'Evil' the
government had erected in the town centre during the
rebellion. Only after the final peace deal was concluded
– years after Riyyak himself had made peace – was the
statue finally dismantled. Now, as the factory owner shook
with rage, Lewis barely flinched. Despite being entirely
preoccupied by the stint of domestic bliss he was currently
enjoying, he had still found time to practise keeping his
cool, suppressing his anger and meditating on the harsh
upbraiding Anami had given him the previous evening. As
predicted, the words had indeed lost their sting; and as luck
would have it, Riyyak even phrased what he said exactly
as Anami had, with nothing added or taken away. Despite
this stroke of luck, the pain in Lewis's knees was worsening
and he felt a violent need to vomit.

'Don't feed me excuses, Nawa. And get ready to serve
the French again, because you're fired.'

Riyyak could grab Lewis by the ears and drag him
across the ground. He could hang him above a boiling
cauldron by his testicles. He could even turn him into a
chair and sit on him. But it was not within his capacity to
fire him. Lewis was confident of this, thanks to a certain
battered old machine that he alone knew how to work.
Even before Riyyak had procured the contraption for the
factory it was already long outdated, and the company that
had manufactured it no longer produced spare parts for it.
Lewis, and no one else, had been able to keep it running
– and that had been with superhuman effort. If he were
fired, it would only be a matter of days before Riyyak
found himself mourning the machine's demise. He had
never enquired of Lewis where he'd learned to service
old-fashioned machinery, as an unskilled factory worker

and former servant. But even if he had, he would have got no response, since Lewis himself did not know.

During the early days of Lewis's long conflict with Tina he had shaved off her hair in a fit of rage one night, while she slept. Tina had then gone to James Riyyak and begged him to take pity on her, but pity was a word whose meaning was entirely foreign to the former rebel. Riyyak guessed she must be the wife of his worker Lewis, since he could smell his particular scent on her body. Riyyak did not mock Tina for her bizarre shorn head. In fact, he found it deeply attractive, supposing the style to be a new feminine trick designed to give a woman an interesting allure. He even wished his own wife had tried it before running away with a Kenyan lorry driver, never to return.

'Do you have some incurable illness? Do you want me to put you out of your misery?' he asked, still baffled as to the kind of pity she had in mind, and seeking recourse to the philosophy of the jungles where he had spent so much of his life.

'No,' she replied, 'my husband Lewis Nawa cut off my hair while I was sleeping and I want you to punish him.'

At that point, the situation became clear and Riyyak realised that, however dazzling it might be, Tina's baldness had nothing whatsoever to do with fashion or a new concept of feminine beauty. Raising his hand, he shooed her away in her weeping state, along with a troublesome fly that had been buzzing around his head.

'Get away with you, woman! Lewis has transformed you into a true Venus, and you don't deserve it one bit.'

Tina did not understand, and nor did anyone else when she repeated the story, including her mother, her uncle Majouk, his dance troupe, and a crowd of local women.

Who was this Venus? Why was Tina unworthy of her? Poor Tina, so firmly convinced of her marred beauty.

In the factory, Lewis was suffering his own woes. Riyyak had turned on his heel and stalked back to his office, barking behind him: 'Now get to work and make something. I need to sign your termination papers.' Dripping with sweat and feeling worse than ever, Lewis stumbled off to his work station. Riyyak's last words were entirely new to him. He'd never heard anything about termination papers before.

FIVE

Having spread death and despair throughout Kinshasa and the surrounding countryside, the wicked sorcerer from Congo had now ensnared Lewis and trailed him back to Nzara. In a few hours Lewis would share the fate of his dear companion Elaine, just as he'd shared the last two passionate years with her; he would join the hundreds of others whose graves he had contemplated pitifully while weeping for his lover and planting purple pansies in the tear-soaked soil.

These were Lewis's disoriented and fearful thoughts as he lay in his colleagues' arms, borne onwards to Nzara's rundown hospital. Riyyak had refused to take him in his jeep, for reasons he alone deemed sound. Firstly, the boss had declared, the vehicle was not a state ambulance and therefore was not to be soiled with blood or other body fluids. Secondly, the patient was no longer a factory employee and therefore was not entitled to pity, having been officially dismissed before his collapse.

Lewis had indeed been dismissed. Upon entering the factory that morning he had failed to notice a huge new machine nestled in a wooden crate and waiting to replace the rickety contraption that had so long guaranteed his protection. Anami had also failed to inform him of this development the previous evening. The situation had come about after Riyyak had finally decided to take the advice of the salesmen who distributed his clothes in neighbouring countries. For some time they had been urging him to increase production so as to meet the massive demand for his cheap clothes, which was growing steadily in line with the rise in poverty. The machine had come specially recommended, and was now waiting to be fired up.

Lewis had a raging fever, and the nausea he had been feeling had now progressed to actual vomit full of blood and bile. His hands and feet were covered in gruesome lesions and the pain in his knees was crippling. Every now and then he was seized by an overwhelming shudder, and passed out completely.

But this piteous scene in the street did not attract much attention, for it was not particularly uncommon. The people of Nzara – and many other towns and cities in the south – were accustomed to such tableaux painted by disease and framed by the harsh realities of poverty. They were used to seeing men collapse into their friends' arms, and women give birth on the way from home to hospital and begin breast-feeding. One year, hysteria had spread through the female population, infecting hairdressers and teachers, European ladies and chieftains' wives and daughters. At the time, it was perfectly common to see a woman prancing topless through the market, or lustfully fondling a papaya tree as if she were seducing her husband. Men grew accustomed to being slapped across the face when enjoying the services of a prostitute in the red light district, or having water hurled at them by a vendor like Tina or her mother, debilitated by the disease.

What made the current scene particularly tragic, however, was the fact that Ebola was behind it. The virus was filled with reckless desire and Lewis was not the only one who would soon be fighting for his life. All those involved were as good as dead.

Although Anami had been infected the previous evening, he still maintained a healthy glow as the virus raged through his elderly blood. Quite unaware of the attack, he continued to shout orders to the men carrying Lewis, in the same nervous tone that had long hindered his promotion.

'Hurry up lads! Come on now – hurry, *hurry*!'

With utter conviction, he reiterated over and over that Lewis was Man of the Year and must be saved at all costs. The men rushed onward, ignoring their own shortness of breath and the stones jabbing their feet. As they advanced, Ruwadi Monti looked down on them with wide cartoon eyes, following their progress from the posters lining the streets.

The town was by no means empty of cars. A number of vehicles, both state and private, were cruising up and down the street, but not a single driver witnessing the scene was tempted to stop and investigate further.

At home, meanwhile, Tina's thoughts were far removed from terror death and blood. She was preoccupied by the idea of fertility at her mature age, and the possibility of becoming pregnant now, given that it had previously proved impossible. What if a miracle truly had occurred and their night of passion had borne fruit, planting a little seed in her belly? In their early years of marriage, her stomach had only ever swollen with phantom infants – and then Lewis had begun his affair, taking his desires to Congo. And now,

after all these years, Tina might soon be rejoicing at a baby's
wails. In a few years' time the child would become the
new man of the house and she would guard him fiercely,
keeping him well hidden from James Riyyak's tyrannous
factory.

Tina had already tried every fertility pill on offer at
the Arab apothecaries, all to no avail. But her neighbour
– the same one who had helped her to hatch the whole
plan – informed her there were new medicines on the
market that had appeared only in the last few years, during
the couple's estrangement. These had apparently helped
countless women, one of whom had conceived triplets.

That morning Tina stretched languidly in bed, imitating
the lethargy of a newlywed weary from a long night of
lovemaking. She bathed in cold water to freshen her skin
and scrubbed herself with a bar of odourless Lifebuoy soap,
well known for its cleansing properties. Once she was dry
she moisturised her face, and mascaraed her eyes, before
heading to the market in search of new remedies. That
evening Lewis would return from his shift exhausted after
many long hours on his feet, and complaining of stiffness
in his legs as he pulled off his grease-stained shirt that was
almost impossible to get clean. Tina would show her husband
no mercy in the bedroom: not because she felt any real
desire for him as such, but because, if they had not already
conceived a child the night before, then the following few
days would be her last opportunity to get pregnant, before
her husband returned to his cheating ways and found yet
another desperate woman to have his way with.

Ebola, meanwhile, was by no means sleeping on the
job. Ever-diligent, it had already infested Tina's blood, bowels
and kidneys. Her otherwise harmless bodily fluids were

now full of the virus, and it lingered in the dirty dishes, in the toilet hole in the middle of the house, and even in Tina's footprints as she headed to the market. If she were not a respectable woman, emotionally fulfilled and preoccupied by her procreative mission, it would also have claimed Mansour, the Arab apothecary. Tina had gone early so as to have unfettered access to the sacks of medicine at the back of his empty shop, and as she entered he began pawing at her face and leaning in for a kiss. Tina did not rebuff him, nor yell in his face. She just gently pushed him away. Her long years of water-selling had acquainted her with every trial and tribulation that could dent the morale of a working woman. After each of the rapes she was subjected to during her work she would grow depressed for a while, but eventually it would fade from her mind and her mood would lift once more. She was used to brutes, and could evade them without so much as raising her voice.

On the recommendations of the spurned apothecary, Tina had bought several grams of Angelica, Monk's Pepper and Maca – the most recent products in stock, he informed her. He instructed her to mix them with lemon juice, in lukewarm water, and to drink one glass a day on an empty stomach. With a glint in his eye that signalled the imminence of another attempted grope, he happily informed her that until the medicine worked its magic she must strive to keep her husband 'pinned to the bed' at all times. Mansour repeated this instruction twice, once in Tina's tribal language, and once in Arabic, which she was fairly fluent in, making it impossible for her not to understand exactly what was implied by 'pinned to the bed.'

Tina headed home, cradling her treasure and tapping her barren belly.

'My sweet Majouk, my beautiful little boy . . . ' She crooned to herself, certain the child would be a boy and she would name him after his folk-dancing uncle. As soon as she reached home she prepared the concoction as instructed by the apothecary and downed the specified dose. Despite having eaten breakfast before going out, she convinced herself her stomach must already be empty.

At that moment there was a knock at the door. It was not her neighbour come to stir up more trouble, as she had expected, nor the homeless orphan she had befriended while experimenting with her emotions. Nor was it her mother, who knew Tina was on leave, having granted it herself. Anami Okiyano was at the door. This was the first time he'd ever knocked on Tina's door so early in the morning, and she guessed he must have come for Lewis, before realising the two men should have both been at work already.

When confronted by unprecedented situations, a person's reactions tend to be dictated by one emotion alone: fear. Snatched from her daydreams, Tina did not bother to ask questions, nor allow Anami to offer a plausible explanation for his presence so early in the day. She panicked. Her ears closed, and Anami's words were rendered futile as she swooned to the dusty ground.

'Lewis isn't dead yet!' Anami yelled, so loudly the crumbling walls shook, the washing line trembled and the muddy floor quaked. But Tina heard nothing.

Anami was entirely unaware of the recent developments in the Nawa household. He knew nothing of Tina's sudden transformation from a conventional wife bent on filling her husband's life with misery into an entirely unconventional one, whose new *raison d'être* was to seduce him and give him a child. Going on his outdated information, Anami was quite bewildered by her reaction. When he described Lewis's grave condition, he had expected joyful ululations to rise up to the papaya trees. Instead, he watched as Tina sank unconscious to the ground.

When drinking with friends, Anami never failed to reiterate his reasons for not marrying. As his head spun with potent arak and contraband Russian vodka he bemoaned the trouble every woman caused – particularly the married ones, who insisted on upholding certain unwritten tenets, such as the commandment that family life be a living hell. In his youth, he had read a self-help book for men, entitled 'Twenty Steps to Happiness.' The book discussed healthy eating and drinking as well as the importance of physical work and a good night's sleep. It even discussed masturbation, and how to dig a grave. Significantly, however, it said nothing of marriage. Thus, whenever Anami's friends chastised him, warning him his name would be lost if he didn't produce children, he would simply remind them of Lewis Nawa and their many other childless friends whose names would also be lost, despite their having endured the daily torment of family life.

With difficulty, Anami roused Tina from what he considered an entirely unnecessary swoon. Despite his sixty years, his back was easily able to bear a woman of seventy kilos, and he was about to lift her up when it struck him that this would attract the unwanted attention of all the neighbours up and down the street. He could already hear the first whispers growing into full-blown gossip. Whilst the tragic spectacle of Lewis's condition might go unnoticed, he and Tina would certainly raise eyebrows. No one would believe she was ill or pregnant, and that he just happened to be passing by at the critical moment. For this reason, Anami abandoned Tina in the small courtyard and hurried to the market, where he hired a donkey cart and two sturdy female corpse washers. When they reached the house the women took over, collecting Tina and continuing to the hospital, where Lewis was sprawled on an examination table, his body infested with the deadly Congolese killer. Both of the hospital's doctors were attending to him, having abandoned an old man to severe and untreatable renal failure, and a baby whose hind quarters remained lodged in its mother's womb as a nurse tried desperately to pull it out. The baby happened to be the first son of a local chieftain, and was therefore about to be announced heir, before it could even begin breastfeeding. If it were to suffocate, not a single medical professional in the town would live to tell the tale.

By this time Ebola was in its element, scoffing delightedly at the might of chieftains and chieftains-to-be. It longed to speak out, to inform everyone they were as good as dead, and there was nothing they could do about it.

Both doctors were local. Nasraddin Akwi was from the Dinka tribe. His face and physique both clearly marked his origins, as did his love for running and the dangers of jungle hunting. In his early youth, however, he had begun to drift away from these Indigenous traditions after an encounter with a Sufi sheikh, while studying in Khartoum; he had converted to Islam soon after that. Luther Ayawo was from the same tribe, but he had had no such change of convictions. Overall, he neither embraced religion nor rejected it; he did not interfere in others' beliefs so long as they did not interfere in his. Both of them were average doctors. They possessed no unusual talents, and were quite incapable of thinking beyond the textbooks they'd studied with every other medical student in the country. Their repertoire included stitching wounds, treating eye infections, and easing difficult births. They could also perform a selection of emergency operations, from Caesarean sections to bowel treatments and reconstructive surgery for the many stab wound victims who passed through the hospital doors. Occasionally, they even tried their hand at extracting bullets from the spines of former rebels, or removing chronic haemorrhoids from the rear ends of men long accustomed to the discomfort they brought. Since Muslims did not consider male circumcision worthy of medical attention this was left to the nurses, who carried it out in their spare moments.

In a brief consultation the doctors agreed that Lewis, writhing feverishly and bleeding from his bowels and his skin, was not suffering from malaria, nor had he contracted typhoid, scarlet fever, relapsing fever or viral dengue fever. In fact, no known fever was likely to cause his skin to dry up and bleed so extensively. They decided to carry out emergency treatments immediately and worry about a diagnosis later. They administered Novalgin via an IV to reduce his temperature, before strapping icepacks to his forehead and feet. Then they called the factory workers in to have their blood tested, taking several pints from anyone matching Lewis's blood group. Throughout these procedures, neither of the doctors, nor the rest of the medical team, donned face masks. The masks were in such short supply they were only used in the operating theatre, and it had not yet occurred to anyone they might be in need of protection. With no idea of what they were battling, they all left themselves open to attack.

Ebola, of course, would not treat the doctors any differently from the rest of the population. Luther and Nasraddin were both treated like kings in Nzara, regardless of their differing religious beliefs. They were used to people stopping them in the street in reverent awe. They were invited to lavish banquets, and had numerous children named after them. Their stories, no matter how stupid, were always applauded, and they were given prime seats at every football match and theatre performance. That very afternoon, they were expected to occupy the two best seats in the stadium and listen to the visiting Congolese guitar player, Ruwadi Monti, aka the Needle.

When Tina arrived at the hospital, accompanied by Anami, the crowd of factory workers broke into applause. No one knew who started it and why the rest followed suit, or what the applause signified. Anami assumed the men had interpreted Tina's arrival as a sign of her willingness to start afresh with her afflicted husband. They were therefore applauding both her and the illness that had reunited the warring couple.

SIX

In sleepy Nzara, where celebrities are few and far between, Ruwadi Monti became an instant hit, stirring the town to life. Tickets for his concert sold like hot cakes, and the various tribes soon began squabbling over them. The black market set up a roaring trade, and the town was filled with the chaotic noise and bustle that a star-studded concert never failed to produce.

From the early morning, Ruwadi prowled the town's busiest thoroughfare, with Darina and the francophone concert organisers in tow. The street was thronging with farmers, factory workers, wandering salesmen and hunters from the nearby jungles. Beggars and orphans lined the pavements, proffering their hands in the hope of a rare gesture of generosity.

Ruwadi spent the day running his hands over the posters on the walls, tracing his disfigured features and dirty, despoiled outfits.

'Have they given me long ears?' he asked Darina. 'Have they cut my hair and changed my beautiful blue suit? Have they given me big eyes to see with?'

Darina replied in the affirmative to his endless stream

of questions and Ruwadi broke into a broad grin, the kind
that usually only appeared when moments of intense joy
caused his thyroid gland to secrete pure hormones into his
bloodstream. His glands were, in fact, rather overactive – he
constantly swung between extremes of happiness and
sadness, necessitating frequent visits to the endocrinologists
of his home country.

'Now I know I have an audience!' he replied in Swahili,
before accosting a procession of donkeys carrying a group
of local primary school teachers to work.

According to Ruwadi's life philosophy, to be criticised
or disfigured is a sign of having successfully attracted the
public's attention. It had taken Ruwadi years to develop
such an attitude, and he now embraced it wholeheartedly.
If his posters had not intrigued people, they would have
remained spotless, untouched and lifeless, leading in turn
to ill-attended and lifeless concerts. Ruwadi was firmly
convinced the graffiti meant that throngs of people –
beautiful women, young men with sleek hair, rich men
with money to burn, and powerful chieftains in need of
famous companions – were preparing to pack the stadium,
ready to boogie to his unique style.

'Dear Sirs,' Ruwadi continued, neatly dodging one of
the donkeys as it lolled its tongue towards his elegant jacket,
'I apologize for interrupting your journey, but tell me: do
you enjoy music?'

'Well, of course!' replied one of the teachers mounted
on the slobbering donkey. Unfortunately, the teacher
continued, neither he nor his companions would be
attending the concert, simply because the average salary of
a local primary school teacher was, at best, just sufficient
to cover the most basic living expenses. Concerts and other

occasional entertainments were affordable only to the lucky few. The teacher expounded at great length on the subject, moving from his personal circumstances to the town as a whole, and going into far more detail than was necessary to quash the hopes of a touring musician. By the time he had finished this painful sermon, Ruwadi's head was spinning terribly. His sightless gaze hovered over the faces of the concert organisers who still had not paid him a penny.

'We'll give you a third of the profits,' they had promised him in advance, 'and we'll take a third too.' Then Ruwadi had been escorted to an uncomfortable hovel, the like of which he had never experienced, even amidst the continent's many civil wars, when every villa and hotel was awash with blood.

If the teacher with the slobbering donkey was to be believed, it seemed the Needle would be walking back to Kinshasa.

One of the organisers attempted to convince him his method of gauging opinion was unreliable at best. Unfortunately, the young men had not yet realised that, no matter how they begged or scolded, they would not stop a man like Ruwadi from pursuing his lifelong habit of accosting strangers. Even as they spoke he was already approaching a group of six women trudging down the road with milk vats on their heads. Ruwadi could tell they were women from the rustle of their dresses, the scent of their homemade perfume and the tap of their feet on the pavement, despite the heavy vats that slightly marred their feminine gait.

'Hello ladies, my name is Ruwadi Monti – are any of you music fans?'

He spoke in French this time, and the milkmaids, who

barely had the will to wash or brush their hair or apply a little cheap mascara to their mournful eyes, completely ignored his foreign babble and continued on their way. They hadn't noticed the posters on the walls, or Ruwadi's sightless eyes. They would barely even have noticed if the moon failed to rise in the sky that night.

It was Anami Okiyano alone who succeeded in restoring a little equilibrium to the musician's troubled soul and, for once, it was not Ruwadi who accosted Anami, but Anami who accosted Ruwadi. He snatched up the musician's hand and almost managed to plant a kiss on it as Ebola surged hungrily through his blood. Ruwadi, however, evaded the gesture by bending down to scratch a thigh that was not remotely itchy.

'It's a great honour to have you perform in our country, sir!' Anami proclaimed in his quick, nervous voice, 'or rather, the country where I currently reside. You are one of Africa's most shining stars! Will you sign my overalls? My name is Anami Okiyano, from Kenya.'

Anami had been on his way to the factory, and was wearing his work clothes. Over the years he had diligently collected the autograph of every celebrity who had ever visited Nzara. He was not particularly interested in their skills or talents, and pursued artists, singers, politicians and activists alike, regardless of whether these last were campaigning for partition or union. The autographs now covered his overalls and, before the guitar player could utter a word, Anami had whipped a special red pen from his pocket, filled with an indelible ink of his own concoction. He handed the pen to the musician and shoved a corner of his sleeve at him, before hurrying off to the factory, dreaming of the splendid evening to come. Anami was familiar with Ruwadi's music, having been to one of his concerts in Nzara before, and listened to the old records his friends owned.

Unfortunately, Anami did not yet realise the evening was not his to spend, since he, like the rest of the town, was marching to the tune of Ebola. It was the deadly Ebola that would decide who listened to Ruwadi and who lay prostrate and bleeding on a hospital bed, as the two doctors desperately sought a cure.

When afternoon came and a loudspeaker in the stadium announced the beginning of the concert, Ruwadi realised his fears of low attendance were unfounded. Entirely oblivious to the fact that Nzara might very well be his final resting place, he began to imagine himself returning home in a gleaming car, with flowers around his neck. A magnificent mahogany chair lined with rhinoceros skin had been carried into the middle of the stadium, and an amplifier with powerful batteries had been connected to Ruwadi's ancient guitar. The organisers instructed him to start a sound check and make sure his strings were sufficiently pliable. At that moment, Ruwadi realised he could smell an audience. He could smell throngs of women in the prime of youth, and men of all ages, even young ones who usually only listened to Jack Alayno or Draydo al-Haddad, whose music seemed to be inspired by the sound of rust being scraped from steel. Ruwadi knew his intuition was correct, and even with perfect vision he could not have appreciated the crowd more.

There were hundreds of girls of different ethnicities and tribes, all of whom had been obsessively practicing their dance moves and were itching to try them out. A feeling of national solidarity filled the stadium. The members of the Nzara folk troupe were present, their legs shaking from the strain of not dancing. They had not been asked to participate and refused to do so without an official invitation, preferring restless legs to wounded pride. Uncle Majouk made light of the matter, loudly extolling the virtues of the traditional brass and leather drum and bamboo *mizmar* the troupe used, and proclaiming them to be far superior to the classical guitar soon to be swept into oblivion by the winds of change. Besides, music alone could not possibly satisfy the audience. Music without singing was like a boat without oars, no matter what the instrument. Unfortunately for Uncle Majouk, however, Ruwadi happened to be among the lucky few who could row without oars and still reach dry land.

Suddenly overcome with the urge to test his instincts, Ruwadi rose to his feet and cleared his throat loudly, before the comely presenter could even begin proceedings.

'I'm Ruwadi Monti! Hello Nzara!' he screamed.

A deafening roar answered his cry, far louder than anything he could have imagined.

'Ruwadi Monti! We love you!'

The calls came from inside the stadium and outside too, where heated skirmishes had broken out between the tribes. The black market had relocated to the main gates and the organisers were being accused of all sorts of dodgy dealing, without any proof of their having stolen a single piaster.

That same day – about two hours after Ruwadi Monti had bustled down the busy street, accosting milkmaids and grumpy school teachers – Tina gained access to the room where her husband was being quarantined. While there, she caught sight of a small section of Lewis's body not blocked by the towering doctors. The man she saw was altogether different to the husband she knew so well, despite their recent estrangement, and Tina went into shock. The way Lewis was shuddering now was quite different to how he had shivered when he had swamp fever. His dark skin was not its usual colour and his sweat had a decidedly unhealthy sheen. It wasn't like him to be lying on his back either; he usually sprawled on his front. When one of the doctors moved away – to fetch something from a cupboard or perhaps to relieve his eyes of the tragic sight – Tina caught a fuller view of Lewis's body. Instantly, she reconciled herself to widowhood.

Her only hope now lay in the previous day's exertions. Could there be a child curled up in her belly? A boy named Majouk, who would live up to all her expectations?

What confused Tina most was the cause of Lewis's sudden illness. She could not recall exactly how he had been when he left the house that morning, since she herself had still been suspended in a euphoric daze. Yet she did remember him picking up his battered old toothbrush and pulling on his grey overalls, just like every other day. The only difference this time was that he had been whistling an old African melody as he did so, and he closed the door softly behind him, something he hadn't done for years. Tina knew his route from home well: he took a shortcut that wound its way through deserted alleyways, empty of news-agents, greengrocers or water-sellers. Not even a chirping bird would have crossed his path on his way to work.

So what had happened to him?

No one knew. Or rather, only Ebola knew, as it feasted on the blood of Lewis and its many other victims, plotting, planning and pouncing whenever possible. Nzara had been a roaring success for the virus. It had particularly enjoyed the textile factory, packed with loud, jostling workers. The marketplace hadn't been too bad either, and nor had the red light district and drinking quarter, the stadium, schools and the high street. In the hospital, meanwhile, Nasraddin Akwi had already fallen into its clutches, soon to be followed by a couple of nurses and a woman in labour.

That evening Anami sat at home alone, weeping bitterly. He had left the hospital, determined to forget Lewis for a few hours and lose himself in Ruwadi's melodies. He had bought his ticket in advance, and joined the long queue waiting to enter the stadium. It was then that Anami was suddenly overcome with dizziness and had to lean on the woman in front of him. Thinking he was groping her, the woman began to call for help. Anami, meanwhile, had broken into a feverish sweat. His nose was running, he could barely breathe, and his knees were aching. He dragged himself home, hoping the walk would refresh him. It did not. Having reached home, he immediately threw up and saw that his vomit was laced with blood. He began to weep. His throat was bleeding, his skin and scalp too. Still crying, he thought of how his sixty years had disappeared in the blink of an eye. He was like a child, wrenched from its mother's womb only to perish before it could even reach her nipple.

No one would come looking for him, since he had never bothered to look for anyone. His drinking companions were friends by night alone, friends who drank arak and contraband vodka with him, then melted away as the sun rose. His colleagues from the factory were either stationed at the hospital, waiting for Lewis to die so they could organise his burial, or at home, dreaming of a lightning bolt to obliterate James Riyyak and his factory.

Everything had become terribly clear to Anami. Lewis was going to die and had dragged him down with him. He told himself over and over again not to be afraid. He must fight, and fight he did, vainly attempting to keep terror at bay. Then, in a moment of good fortune, one of his neighbours came looking for a cup of sugar, having been surprised by the arrival of unexpected guests. She knew Anami always had some in the cupboard, since it was his habit to drink a cup of sugar water every day. This, he claimed, was the secret to his perennial strength and vitality.

SEVEN

The following day, the word 'epidemic' began to echo through the hospital. At first it did so silently, in the anxious minds of the doctors. But soon they began to whisper it to one another, and it was not long before the whole hospital was buzzing with the word, from the nurses and cleaners to the visitors and the unemployed lounging in the neglected garden.

Epidemic . . . epidemic . . . epidemic.

The previous evening, Anami Okiyano had arrived on a donkey loaned from a local charity worker. Around the same time, a tavern owner from the bar district was brought in, the same woman who had stolen a fateful, drunken kiss from Lewis as he returned from Kinshasa. The next after-noon they were joined by two of the factory workers who had helped transport Lewis to hospital.

Meanwhile, Manko Nokosho, one of Nzara's best-loved and most handsome residents, was adamantly refusing to be treated. He had no idea how he had been infected, but fiercely resisted any attempts to load him onto a donkey and parade him through the streets. The donkey's poor back would surely buckle beneath his considerable weight and, all in all, he preferred to die contentedly in his shop, still clutching the razor that had not left his side for fifty years.

The whisper is among the most ancient of traits particular to far-flung towns. In such societies, many a successful deal is conducted in whispers, and a particularly well-cooked whisper, seasoned with carefully chosen words, can gain a great following. In times of distress, when all other entertainment fails, whispers often become the most valuable commodity.

And so the whispers had begun to emanate from the hospital where Lewis and the other more recent victims lay. Some of the mutterings put a comic spin on events, others tended to melodrama, and some were simply bleak.

In the market, the Arab merchants refused to take any notice of the grim whispers hinting at a foreign epidemic that was both incurable and fatal. The Arabs had monopolised trade for decades, ever since the days when their shops were filled with slaves, woven bark shoes and dyed rooster feathers. Now, they had no intention of locking up the businesses their fathers had left them and abandoning their sole source of livelihood, of settling their accounts, shredding their debt books and hurrying from the town, as empty-handed as their ancestors had first arrived there.

The town's prostitutes and local brewers – who made their wine from maize, barley and coffee beans – had no time for such whispers either. Heeding the rumours would have required the women to obey the laws of cleanliness and purity, cease their seductive trade and guard their bodies from anyone unfamiliar. They would also have been obliged to take the morals of the situation into account, so as to protect the town's population from perishing in a state of filth and intoxication. But the women refused to submit to the basic laws of survival, and were deaf to the warnings of certain death predicted by the whispers. Without ever articulating it to one another, their collective decision was to pursue the path of depravity until the very end.

'The life of a working girl is far harder than any death' they repeated amongst themselves, not certain which of them had first uttered these heartening words.

The factory workers, meanwhile, were taken in by the more comedic whispers, one of which claimed the mysterious illness only affected monkeys, and so anyone who caught it must therefore be a monkey. In order to distract themselves and relieve their growing anxiety as more and more of their colleagues fell ill, they began checking each other's behinds for a suspect tail, declaring that Lewis had certainly possessed one and that Anami, like all monkeys, had had a particular weakness for bananas. One worker even dashed off to Anami's machine, returning seconds later with a pile of dry brown peels.

Only James Riyyak remained despondent. For the first time since opening the factory, he had begun to entertain the possibility of failure. Both his studies in Uganda and his time in the jungle had taught him that a shepherd must keep a close eye on his flock at all times. Thus he pored over the factory register containing the names, shifts and salaries of every employee. In his hand he brandished the pen, both literal and metaphorical, that allowed him to add and erase as he saw fit. Lewis Nawa had already been eliminated by the new machine, followed by his strange illness. In any case, he was no loss, Riyyak reflected with a shake of the head. Anami, meanwhile, was a terribly nervy fellow. He could be provoked by the tiniest mosquito buzzing in his ear and, whenever Riyyak had considered promoting him to Foreman or Assistant Manager, he'd hesitated and eventually decided against it. But Anami was still an essential part of factory life, like raw cotton, cooling tubes, or the lorry that delivered new clothes to the marketplace. Riyyak would not erase Anami's name until he was certain he would not come bustling through the door again. As for the rest of the infected men, they were everyday workers with no specialist skills. But their loss would still affect business.

Riyyak wandered through the rows of machines, giving a fond pat to those in working order and cursing any that had ground to a halt. Several times he yelled at the workers, too, ordering them away from one another's backsides and urging them to exercise greater caution in protecting themselves from harm. As he did so, a crazy thought occurred to him and a broad grin instantly spread across his face: masks! The town needed face masks.

That afternoon, Riyyak sat down at his table to resurrect his long-neglected talent for drawing. He had abandoned the pursuit in his youth, deeming it futile and indulgent. Riyyak was a skilled artist and had once been in the habit of depicting the faces of well-known colonialists embellished with snake eyes, parrot beaks and chimpanzee ears. One of his oil paintings had even won an award and been hung in the Red Cross building before it was destroyed in the war. His other favourite subject was a young English girl, for whom he had harboured a depraved sort of love that he did not dare to confess.

Riyyak's hand began to move across the paper, sketching various designs for a face mask composed of layers of protective cotton gauze. The final pattern was completed in record time and immediately passed to the production line. By the following day, the shops of Nzara would be filled with Riyyak Masks.

But there were a good many things that Riyyak did not know about Ebola. Among them was the fact that the deadly virus had already taken possession of a large number of his employees, who now gave this ruthless killer access to a store of live ammunition – from their absolutely basic toilet facilities to the filthy roads they trod, the ingredients of their meals and, above all, their firm belief that it was a wicked sorcerer who was spreading death through the town.

Meanwhile, Lewis had woken from his coma in a small, blood-stained hospital room littered with syringes and thick with the smell of disinfectant. He was now experiencing what was known locally as the 'deathbed awakening,' although nobody could ascertain whether the name exactly fitted the phenomenon. Lewis's temperature was back to normal and the rash covering his skin had begun to fade. Now that his tongue was back in working order, he had also grown rather bold. He was busy cursing, struggling with the nurses and cracking dirty jokes while his hands furiously scratched his head and his legs frantically kicked the blanket from the bed.

No one had been present to witness Lewis's sudden return to lucidity. Both doctors were hurrying back and forth between their patients, attending to Anami and all the others that had arrived that day. Nasraddin had also become infected, although he did not yet know it. The idea of face masks had briefly crossed his mind, but was soon swept aside by another moan of distress.

Lewis managed to attract the attention of a nurse rushing past. She peered at him cautiously, and was about to run and fetch a doctor when Lewis began to reel off the dishes he felt like eating – all the usual kinds of fare to be found in the basket of a hospital visitor. Luckily for him, those very dishes were in fact packed snugly in the hamper Tina had just brought from home. She too was beginning to feel slightly unwell, but had convinced herself it was merely the combination of fatigue and concern for her dying husband.

Lewis began to eat and drink heartily, belching loudly and taking full advantage of his deathbed awakening. If the ward had not been so crowded, and therefore completely devoid of privacy, he would also have attempted to identify an unfussy nurse whose fancy he might tickle before dying.

Tina remained motionless. Having resigned herself to a life of widowhood, she was utterly disorientated by Lewis's recovery. To add insult to injury Lewis then broadcasted, at full volume, that he had been cheating on her for the past two years.

This confession was no news to Tina, of course – she had known about his adultery right from the start, from the first mild flirtation right the way through to his lover's death, his copious tears and the purple pansies he planted on her grave. But she feigned astonishment, glancing over at her mother, who had decided to take enough time off work to be with her daughter until the corpse was buried and the mourning concluded.

'You've been having an affair?'

'Yes, with Elaina. *And* Kanini – I met Kanini a few days ago,' declared Lewis, raising his finger and pointing it in his wife's face, 'and I would've happily cheated on you with anyone else, until that damn sorcerer got me!'

One of the unfortunate effects of a deathbed awakening is that it prompts people to quite suddenly air their dirty laundry, assuming death will soon obliterate it forever. Yet on occasion these awakenings are not followed by death, but simply represent a return to consciousness, after which the confessors must live the rest of their lives in a state of guilty repentance.

Unbeknown to Lewis and all those present, Ebola also has a peculiar habit of occasionally sparing its victims. The reason for this aberrance in its otherwise destructive nature remains a mystery. Perhaps Lewis's robust immune system had simply sapped the virus and forced it from his blood. Or perhaps it was down to something more mysterious. Whatever the case, Lewis Nawa was not experiencing a deathbed awakening; he was simply on the mend.

Lewis's words were met with a startled gasp from everyone present. Doctors, nurses and nosy onlookers who had managed to slip past the barriers and crowd round Lewis's bed all took a deep breath, drawing in the stale air.

Tina wept, not because of Lewis's past infidelity, but because of his intention of resuming it. What's more, he had ruined all the plans she'd formulated for her newfound widowhood: the tears she'd been storing up and the long period of mourning she'd been anticipating. Lewis had ruined everything.

At that moment a nurse ran into the room with fresh news – relieving the uncomfortable tension a little, but adding to the general sense of doom.

Anami Okiyano had passed away, along with the tavern owner and one of the factory workers. A pigeon had also died after crashing into one of the hospital windows.

EIGHT

Contagion. Unstoppable, deadly contagion.

Everything in the town pointed to this fact.

Everything screamed it, loud and clear.

In the market, all commerce had ground to a halt. Only a handful of traders remained, refusing to heed the panicked whispers and obstinately pursuing their greedy struggle. They stood beneath their awnings, gazing in consternation at the empty surroundings.

In the industrial quarter, an air of stagnation lay over the factories. Riyyak's operation was the sole hive of activity – continuously churning out face masks.

Endless scenes of tragedy now filled the streets: invalids carried aloft, carted by donkeys, or simply dragged over the rough ground. Schools and government offices had been abandoned, and all those with the means and the will were preparing to flee before the borders closed and the town was cut off from the outside world.

The outbreak had far exceeded the limited capacity of the hospital: never before had it been faced with such an epidemic. Luther was now working alone, since Nasraddin Akwi had eventually been carried home to die in peace, far from the sordid rants that echoed through the hospital corridors. To compensate for the hospital's shortages thousands of mattresses stuffed with straw, cotton and sand had been spread out in one of the town squares, the very same place where rebels had once mulled over their wartime woes, and Lewis Nawa had been crowned Man of the Year.

The last IVs were hooked into bleeding arms and every available scrap of cloth draped over a feverish brow. Now the Novalgin had run out, this was the only way to lower temperatures. Gone were all semblances of care and tenderness. Gone were all attempts at decent, dignified burials. Such things were luxuries in the time of Ebola.

The Congolese government had finally released the identity of the mysterious virus that had been hounding the country for so long now. The announcement was made by a Doctor Ngoy Mushola, who claimed to have discovered it and named it Ebola after a small river that ran through the villages of the Kikwit region. It was there that the virus had made its first, tentative appearance, bringing down an elderly lumberjack, and then his family and close friends. In his announcement, the doctor discussed the physical composition of the virus, emphasising its ability to lie dormant, and the ferocity of the outbreak that could follow. He went on to explain how the virus multiplied rapidly in the patient's blood, thereby causing his or her collapse. After infection, it was possible, but very rare, that certain people might survive.

In his final statement, the doctor described the victims' deaths as the most excruciating known to man, a judgment that made Ebola immensely happy.

A snap decision was then made to close the Congolese border, the government having been inspired with the kind of zeal that often leads to political activists having their eyes gouged out or power-crazed politicians being shot or hung in public squares. Following this, in a tone of utmost optimism, the authorities announced that the situation was now under control.

Meanwhile, the country's more scientifically minded citizens were torn between a desire to laugh in triumph and quake with fear, now that their incessant warnings about the virus had been proved right. Their jaws still ached from their tireless attempts to caution their fellow country-men. On the other hand many chieftains had fallen from grace, as their sorcerers – sent to remote corners of the country armed with talismans – had achieved nothing, and the tribesmen were now demanding the return of loved ones lost to a medical illness and not a wicked magician.

A dignified chieftain, walking anxiously through the village, would be tripped up by a protruding foot. Children, previously terrified of their leader, now had no qualms about screaming at him, demanding their mother's return.

Like in many African countries, there was no shortage of wicked sorcerers in Congo, all specialists in spilling blood, sabotaging childbirth and, in general, doing death's dirty work. Firmly convinced the outbreak was the work of a fellow sorcerer, they simply dreamed of possessing his supe-rior skills.

Closing the borders did nothing to prevent the spread of terror. No amount of ruthlessness and menacing guns could deter Ebola's victims. They had resolved to meet their death at the hands of slavish border guards, and that was how they would meet it.

Caravans of refugees spread north and south, east and west. One group was even heading for Nzara, blithely unaware that Ebola had beaten it across the border in the blood of a certain factory worker. The train of barefoot travellers was scattered and fearful, ill-equipped for the journey, with only a few cars and donkeys. Among its number were several rather controversial figures: a couple of veteran athletes, a few ex-ministers deposed after embezzling public funds, and several mavericks who had had to give up their usual nocturnal existence of deprivation and self-denial – including the great magician, Jamadi Ahmed. Having abandoned his eponymous street because of Lewis, he was now heading to Lewis's homeland, the last place on Earth where a terrified magician, clinging to life, might expect to find relief. What most irked Jamadi, however, was the complete lack of interest displayed by the other occupants of his car. He'd performed several classic tricks to whet their appetite, but they had all remained impassive, even the old crone whose marriage proposal he had rejected forty years ago and who had attended his performances ever since, right up until that final show when she had watched in amazement as the enraged Jamadi disappeared into the city streets.

Back in Nzara, Ruwadi had also been informed about the epidemic ravaging the city. His faithful companion Darina had broken the news, cowering in a corner of their miserable hovel so as to reduce their chances of spreading the disease to one another. The francophone concert organisers had repeated her words, coming and going in hushed whispers, and occasionally kicking the room's messy furniture around in frustration. At this Ruwadi's thyroid gland went into overdrive. His eyes popped hysterically, his heart pounded, and his fingers trembled so uncontrollably that when he strummed the guitar it was impossible to distinguish his familiar old melodies from his more recent compositions. His roars of rage now met only with scorn from the organisers. In their eyes, he was no longer a star who must be humoured but a dead man walking, just like the rest of them.

'We've made a great profit, lads,' Ruwadi yelled, 'so let's spruce up this miserable hostel. I loathe it. I want a bath and a fan that doesn't keep me up all night with its racket. I want Imperial Leather soap and shampoo. Darina, Darina, did any of those mangy dogs manage to kiss me during the concert? Tell me, did anyone take my hand, or breathe into my face? Were that girl's cheeks feverish? The one who threw hair at me?'

Ruwadi was the greatest nuisance in Darina's life. Once upon a time, she had enjoyed his annoying interjections, and would even nag him to say something during his rare moments of calm introspection. Ruwadi had moulded Darina, a defenceless and rootless orphan, plucking her from the street where she would otherwise have grown up to eventually become part of its sinful fabric. Ruwadi had given her a perfectly normal upbringing: nutritious food, clean clothes, and a little education and training in etiquette. It was entirely of her own accord that she had become his permanent walking stick.

Another of Ruwadi's numerous life philosophies was that true artists must be wedded to their art alone. Neither of his previous marriages had succeeded in shaking this conviction, both ending swiftly in divorce. Two years previously, the subject had been raised by a female journalist while Ruwadi was visiting a neighbouring county. He was attending the inauguration ceremony of an army officer whose successful coup had led to him being named president for life. Without so much as a twinge of his conscience,

Ruwadi had accepted a fee to entertain and, during the ceremony, a young female journalist had accosted him. From the tone of her voice he could tell she must work for a tabloid, and Darina later told him that the woman had removed both her shirt and bra during the interview, under the pretext of the intense heat.

'Mr Monti,' she'd addressed him, 'Do you lead some kind of secret life on that farm of yours, with your cattle and your parrots? I've heard you enjoy the company of beasts.'

'Yes,' had been his swift reply, 'I have a female donkey who keeps me in good cheer.'

Sweeping aside these memories, Darina retreated into her corner, vaguely fanning the air as though to fend off an invisible threat. The bloody images she'd witnessed in the rebels' square that morning flashed before her: corpses, syringes, decay. Horrors that had made her heart pound painfully against her ribs. She thought miserably of how quickly her short life had ended, before she could prove herself worthy of marrying and raising a family. Now she would never inherit Ruwadi's house, or the farm outside Kinshasa where he kept parrots, dogs and racehorses. They would die together in a town that was supposed to bring them great profits, not certain death.

Darina realised she was crying and could not bring herself to answer any of Ruwadi's frenzied questions.

'When are you planning to take us home, lads?' he suddenly yelled, addressing the agitated organisers as a rush of hormones made his teeth chatter wildly and his bushy moustache quiver. His white hair – which Darina usually combed and shined with Vaseline more than three times a day – was now a tousled mess, unfit for a refined artist such as himself. He strummed his guitar, capable of producing only the most discordant of melodies.

One of the francophone organisers managed to silence Ruwadi by bringing him a small radio tuned to RTNC, the Congolese national radio station. The channel churned out fresh information about the virus: how many had died that day, the areas of Kinshasa likely to be struck next, the opinions of the doctor who'd discovered it, the possibility of a cure . . .

'Listen here,' Ruwadi began to bluster, but the young man cut him off with 'This is the situation in your country!' and Ruwadi fell silent. His tongue froze, and his ancient guitar dropped to the floor. Then suddenly he remembered how a factory worker had touched his hand that morning, and would have planted a kiss on his cheek had Ruwadi not ducked in time, smelling the unappealing odours of his approaching mouth. He remained silent, afraid of what he might hear if he asked about the worker. His thoughts wandered frantically over the possible outcomes of his predicament. It seemed unlikely he would escape unscathed, but, for now, he still had a healthy tongue and a set of fingers fit to strum. With the extreme precautions he took over his health, he also doubted any contagion could get the better of him. Besides, Anami had barely even brushed against him. Ruwadi would not have even noticed were it not for his extraordinary sense of touch.

Meanwhile, James Riyyak had succeeded in producing his masks in a single night. Every employee fit to work had been commissioned, and Riyyak himself had inspected their health, darting frantically from machine to machine, and submitting the men to a long interrogation about what they'd eaten and drunk over the last two days, and who they'd been with. Business was soon thriving in the affluent and the impoverished parts of town alike, with the help of his trusty child workers. He also lowered the cost of the masks so that even beggars, servants and lepers could afford them – these last now suddenly appearing to be in glowing health in comparison to the victims of Ebola. In order to market his product to those who still adhered to traditional Indigenous faiths, and were therefore praying to the gods of fire, wood and trees for mercy from the illness, Riyyak daubed various patterns of his own design onto the masks, claiming they were protective talismans.

Riyyak was fearless in the face of Ebola, viewing it as just one more affliction he would have to overcome in the course of his life. He'd already had several near-death experiences, the most spectacular of which had involved him plummeting to earth in a helicopter during the days of the rebellion. Riyyak had pinched the helicopter from under the nose of the national army and taken to the air, despite having no knowledge of piloting. There had been another close shave when his wife served him a dish of fresh gazelle meat laced with rat poison, just before she ran off with the Kenyan lorry driver. For once, he hadn't been hungry, however, and when he discovered his wife's cowardly flight the next day and smelled poison in the rotting meat, he grew convinced he must be one very lucky devil. With that same conviction, Riyyak now decided the deadly virus would not strike him.

As he rumbled through the town in his jeep touting his talismanic masks to any residents he deemed likely to believe in them, Riyyak posed himself – and answered – a few quick-fire questions concerning death and destruction:

'What's worse: a burning helicopter or Ebola?'

'A burning helicopter, of course.'

'What's worse: rat poison or Ebola?'

'Rat poison, of course.'

'What's worse: a Molotov cocktail in the hands of a brainless government soldier or Ebola?'

'A Molotov cocktail, of course.'

With overblown faith in his own good luck, Riyyak failed to realise Ebola was not a lone assassin that he could cleverly out-manoeuvre. Nor did it compare to his helicopter crashing into a sturdy tree and becoming lodged in a dense tangle of branches, or a plate of poisoned meat left untouched by chance. Ebola was all around, accompanying him on his sales trips and silently mocking his masks and supposed luck. Millions of mini-viruses were already busying themselves in the posh end of town where the foreigners lived, a community made up of aid workers, educational consultants who trained the locals, and devout Christians striving to restore the former glory of their missions. In addition, there was the odd wandering traveller – there for no specific purpose – and a few artists who found such a primitive society an exotic source of inspiration.

NINE

Lewis Nawa soon faded into insignificance now that chaos had seized the city. The little hospital room he was occupying for the fourth consecutive day was no longer the centre of anyone's attention. It seemed a rare opportunity had come Lewis's way to become an urban legend; the man who survived the very disease he had brought to the city, while so many others had perished. And yet it was not to be. Lewis's story met with little enthusiasm from the people who happened to recognise him amidst the chaos outside, as the battle raged on between life and death – a battle he had started and then escaped. Yet even Lewis wasn't entirely safe: the virus may have released him this time, but there was nothing to say it wouldn't return at any moment.

Were this not the time of Ebola, Lewis's life story – gabbled out during what he had thought to be his deathbed awakening – would have become the hottest news in town, on the lips of every citizen, friends and strangers alike. A cautionary tale for any woman rushing into marriage simply because a passer-by asked for her hand.

Things would have turned out very differently for Tina, too. She would have ignored her interfering neighbour and reinstated the old rocks to their position in the doorway. She might even have added an extra jagged one close by to crack Lewis's skull open as he stumbled in. Perhaps Tina would even have gone back to Mansour, the apothecary, to return the fertility remedies she had just bought. This time she might have let Mansour casually grope her. After all, Lewis's regular infidelity during their long estrangement was one thing, but his intention to deceive her again, after everything she'd gone through, was too much to bear.

As it happened, Tina hadn't time for any of this, not even to scratch her head in confusion. Those present at her deathbed awakening heard how she had purchased a hatchet from an ironmonger, intending to put it to the worst of uses, before returning it in a burst of guilty conscience. She spoke also of the local teenagers who ran about the neighbourhood barefoot, playing football. She had so longed to seduce them, to teach them how to touch a female body, savour a kiss, and work around society's moral code, no matter how concrete it seemed. It was only for her own sake that she abandoned the idea. Perhaps she also mentioned being raped in her youth and how her husband had abandoned her immediately after, yet nobody listening could make out exactly what Tina was saying.

'If I hadn't been a water-seller, I'd have been a dancer in the Nzara Folk Dance Troupe, with my uncle, Majouk.' This was the last phrase Tina's spectators were certain they heard her say. The words were the opposite of the response she normally gave when asked the age-old question, 'If you weren't you, who would you be?' To which, of course, her standard response was, 'I would be me.'

Tina's mother, who went by the common name of Ashoul and was now in her fifty-ninth year, stayed by her daughter's side until the very end. She was there to wipe the sweat and blood from her brow and watch, in a stupor, the steady drip of the IV into her arm. During all this, she flatly refused to wear the Riyyak Mask that Majouk had given her, vehemently declaring that the soul of her departed husband – hovering forever close by, in times of joy and sorrow alike – wanted both wife and daughter back by his side.

'Come to me, Ashoul. Please, come to me with Tina. I've missed you both so much . . .'

Uncle Majouk was weeping behind his mask, which was already wet through, not because it was poorly made – Riyyak's products were expertly constructed, despite the hasty manufacturing the situation had dictated – but because his tears were so copious. Tina had gone. Her eyes were still open and her dry tongue lolled from her mouth. At that point, now that the time had come for her daughter to be buried in the mass grave the authorities had assigned to Ebola's victims – people of all races and creeds slung in together, without time spared for them to be bathed or covered – Tina's mother turned to her brother Majouk and begged, 'Please don't let me have a deathbed awakening, Majouk. If I come round like that, I want you to strangle me. I've so much resentment for you locked up inside me, and I don't want you to hear it. I mean it, Majouk, please.' Majouk was not enough of an artist to be celebrated after he was gone, particularly in a town marching quickly towards its demise, where no one's memory was likely to live on. Forty years of leaps, twists and leg strain were rewarded by no more than the occasional smile from a small group of old ladies who would forget him a few days later, a box of contraband Cuban cigars from a Congolese fan, and a certificate of achievement from the head teacher of his primary school, awarded after a certain amount of bribery from the leaders of his tribe. Majouk had mounted the certificate on a wall in the room where he lived alone, positioned next to a pair of bulls' horns, a string of beads and an antique set of armour he wore while performing. He would inspect these possessions obsessively every time he entered or left the room. Majouk didn't even own a kettle or a cooking pot, and the little room was host to only the most meagre selection of memories, which he would gather together in his head whenever alone.

Ashoul was not the only one harbouring bitter thoughts about Majouk. To prevent his misdeeds from emerging in someone else's deathbed awakening he would have had to strangle every woman in the local brothel, since all had experienced his sadistic attitude towards women such as themselves while they strived to please him and conceal their loathing. He would have had to suffocate the barmaids in the taverns too, where he had a reputation as the vilest drunkard ever to stagger through their doors. A notorious fight-starter, he was always looking for the next ruckus and had spilled much young blood in his time. His dance companions would have had to go too, given how often he had called in on them at home just to gawp unashamedly at their wives. And finally, he would have had to hang himself. After all, who knows one's own dark secrets better than oneself?

Once Ebola had got to his sister, Uncle Majouk just about managed − in his befuddled state − to tie her hands and feet to her sickbed. The time for Ashoul's deathbed awakening had come. With a large scrap of muslin scrounged from a neighbouring room, he smothered her swollen mouth as it struggled to utter all manner of obscene anecdotes.

Afterwards, he exchanged his sodden mask for three new ones, all branded with talismans (for Majouk was ever faithful to his ancestral spirits). Then he carried his sister on his back to the mass grave and threw her in beside her daughter.

Task complete, Majouk returned to his room and gazed at the certificate gained through such determined effort. He hated it. Tearing off every one of his face masks, he threw them to the ground, stomped on them and began to wail. It was as if he could hear the spirit of his brother-in-law, Azacouri, calling him closer, radiating waves of longing and reminding him of the days when they would play straw-ball together in the alley. And the time when, as teenagers, they had cruelly ensnared a wild ass in the forest, then sold it to an Arab tradesman. His memories were of little interest to anyone in that town he held so dear, where he had spent his whole life dancing tirelessly to the Kambala, Shoushounka and Touniji. Majouk stretched out on the old wooden bed and closed his eyes. At a time when Ebola was savagely claiming one life after another, Majouk was the only person to die of heart failure. Plain old boring heart failure.

Meanwhile, Lewis had finally made his way out of the hospital room, flexing his arms and legs as if warming up for a run, still wearing the grubby white sheet his colleagues had wrapped him in as they rushed him to hospital in that most tragic of tableaux.

Lewis's first port of call was the empty hospital canteen, formerly staffed by local cooks with very little cooking ability. In most cases, they couldn't even distinguish between the food appropriate for cancer patients, heart attack victims and cirrhosis sufferers, and that required by hunters, lorry drivers and street hawkers. Lewis was hungry. The deliveries of homemade meals from his colleagues had ceased now that the epidemic had spread and the local people had fled for their lives. Lewis had no idea that Tina had been hit; that she had awoken one last time for her ungodly deathbed awakening and then passed away. Nor was he aware that Tina's mother had also succumbed, and that Majouk, the unremarkable folk dancer and last remaining member of his ill-fated family, was currently demonstrating the behaviour of a well-mannered corpse, having been covered where he lay by his colleagues. They had happened to pay Majouk an uncustomary visit that same day, calling to consult him – as the most senior of the dancers – about whether the troupe's brass and leather drums could also fall victim to the mysterious disease.

In the kitchen, Lewis came across a box of English-style wafers, a shoddy knock-off manufactured in Kinshasa. The biscuits had belonged to a nurse who suffered from spells of low blood sugar, but when terror struck they had been forgotten completely. Besides these, Lewis also found a bottle of potent coffee bean wine belonging to one of the cooks who sold it on to the hospital's inpatients. The cook must have fallen ill before having the chance to hide it. After all, the discovery of a bottle like that in a government institution would spark a whole host of probing questions for which answers would be demanded – if there were even enough officials left to form an investigative committee, that is. There was nothing else to be found, other than a few cockroaches, resiliently defying the lack of sustenance, several lizards investigating the situation from cracks in the wall before darting back inside, and a tangle of spiders' webs dangling from the soot-smeared ceiling.

As he devoured the nurse's biscuits and gulped the wine

straight from the bottle, Lewis realised he was being observed hungrily through the broken window by a beady-eyed cat. Unnerved, he wandered off through the hospital corridors, peering tentatively around and venturing into the now deserted wards. Instantly intoxicated by the wine, he entirely forgot he and his country were in the midst of a crisis, and casually tripped into the operating theatre, the site of many a botched surgery. He placed a dirty pillow on the operating table and opened it up with a scalpel, guffawing all the while and uttering the sorts of bawdy phrases that would never enter a surgeon's mind while cutting open a patient's stomach or repairing a haemorrhage.

Lewis felt no regret for having aired his dirty laundry during what he had mistakenly reckoned to be his deathbed awakening. In fact, he still half hoped to come across some wretched girl with whom he could pursue his infidelity, which had now become second nature to him. For some reason, Kanini had suddenly returned to his thoughts. Kanini, who had kept him at it for two days straight, erasing his grief for Elaine and sending him back to Nzara with raging hormones. Kanini, who for some mysterious reason now appeared far more delectable than Elaine and Tina put together. Through all this, Lewis had no sense of the many reasons why he should have died after that painful awakening, the most significant being that, having brought the murderous virus to the city, he was now considered its chief accomplice.

Kanini, meanwhile, no longer existed anywhere other than in Lewis's imagination. When he'd left her that day – under the pretence of going to collect the money she needed to pay her debts – she hadn't hung around for long before forgetting all about him and going off in search of another man to win her confidence and then deceive her. This was the pattern of events Kanini had known ever since leaving the countryside for a merciless city which had not a speck of compassion in its heart for a wandering orphan or, more precisely, for a lost cause of a woman such as herself.

Lewis could picture Kanini clearly, recalling her beauty in exact detail and comparing it to that of his two other women. Had he the slightest talent for drawing he would have sat down and sketched her in full, stark naked and absorbed in the ecstasy of the moment. Kanini, however, did not remember Lewis at all. Partly because the memory of a prostitute is similar, in many ways, to that of a dictator – clouded by sin and depravity – but mainly, because Kanini was dead. She had died the same day she had gone out to loiter in the streets in search of a new foreigner, killed not by Ebola – the virus was spreading its way through her body slowly and had not yet decided to bring her down – but in the course of her work.

The toxic street where Kanini loitered that time was nothing like the sophisticated Jamadi Ahmed Street where she had first spotted Lewis. Here, a man stopped her and asked for her name. This was a common opening and Kanini immediately made something up, as was usual practice. She had always thought she might divulge her real name once some trust had been established, but this was something that had never happened. There was simply no trust to be found in the profession of selling one's body, neither for seller nor punter. The list of debts that had provoked Lewis's flight was still in Kanini's handbag, along with some cheap cases of make-up, essentials in a profession that depends on three things: a perfectly made-up face, an agile body, and a flexible set of morals.

Of course even Kanini was not her real name, the one used and abused back on the farm by the local teenagers and the horse owners and trainers, but it was the one she usually liked to use in Kinshasa. Of course she hadn't told Lewis Nawa her real name, and she didn't even tell him her city name, until he teased it out of her after extending his visit. On this occasion, Kanini told the stranger her name was Diyani Joy, laughing as if to prove it. The stranger was well-built, with a smiling, clean-shaven face and a silver earring in his left ear. He had more the look of a slick pimp than that of an ordinary customer, and this excited Kanini greatly. For all those years in Kinshasa, she had searched in vain for an intermediary to make her life a little easier. She had knocked on the doors of all the well-known brothels, only for the matrons to praise her youth, beauty and allure before rejecting her apologetically, claiming that the house was already overcrowded, with all the comings and goings the work entailed. The men who managed brothels remotely – some of whom she had managed to track down – were not taken by her either, preferring the sort of girls seen splashed across travel brochures. When the stranger grabbed her by the wrist, checked her pulse and felt the veins throbbing in her neck, Kanini was thrilled. The man groped her hungrily then told her to have a thorough wash, as today was the day she would meet her death at the hands of him and his friends, who were waiting nearby. Kanini laughed. The phrase 'death at my hands' was a common expression in the industry, uttered by all sorts of clientele, from the self-proclaimed studs to those crippled by self-loathing. Most of the time the words turned out to be utterly empty, once a deal had been struck and they got down to business. In the meantime, Kanini had already darted off to a public toilet where she washed herself and checked the state of her eyebrows, fake eyelashes and cheap lipstick. Then she accompanied the stranger to a sinister-looking wasteland behind the main streets where a crowd of dazed and dishevelled men and women were gathered. As soon as she arrived, the crowd surrounded her frantically. Kanini screamed, but it was much too late for that.

And so it was that Kanini, the wayward country girl, became the latest name on the list of people to die needlessly – for the simple reason that the world is home to peculiar folk who enjoy gratuitous slaughter. Perhaps if she had survived until Ebola had taken her she wouldn't have been chopped into pieces and dumped in some bin.

TEN

Lewis Nawa left the hospital still wearing his inpatient's gown, which covered only the top half of his body and left the bottom half naked but for a thick coat of body hair, a few mosquito bites and a wealth of lesions left by Ebola that were now beginning to heal over.

The streets were dusty, baking in the midday August sun, and there wasn't even a scent of the equatorial rain that usually fell the whole year round. Yet the town was not completely deserted. A few traders hurried past, their faces covered by Riyyak Masks. Ebola's tragic victims were evident all around. With no one left to carry them, they crawled alone to the main square in the hope of finding help. Lewis, meanwhile, was completely oblivious to his bare feet, already blistering as they pounded the baking road. Any feeling – including that of a guilty conscience – had been entirely deadened by the bottle of coffee bean wine he had guzzled.

The image of Kanini, naked and bashful, had also faded from his mind, along with all other friends, lovers and acquaintances: Tina, her mother, Uncle Majouk, Anami Okiyano, Elaine . . . Instead, his head was filled with gruesome visions of James Riyyak: a variety of imaginary scenarios he and his workmates had long delighted in. Often, they included Riyyak being tied to a giant papaya tree, his body peppered with stab wounds. Lewis was no killer, and had never harboured actual murderous intentions before, not even towards the mice that scurried into his house, the annoying pups that rubbed against his legs or the neighbour's cheeky cat that sometimes made off with his dinner. And as he entertained these thoughts, Lewis was not even aware that Riyyak had relieved him of his employment the previous day, and had then refused to take him to hospital in his jeep. Lewis had collapsed before he could learn any of that and, since Ebola had then taken Anami, he would never discover the truth. Perhaps it was the potent wine inspiring such murderous impulses in him, or perhaps the virus had damaged some of his brain cells, causing him to lose his sense of reason and propriety as he impassively observed the zombie-like people crowding the streets. Picking a few masks up from the ground he inspected them thoroughly for traces of blood and mucus, sniffing for any whiff of the rancid odour he'd smelled on himself before falling ill. Finding none of these, Lewis donned all of the masks at once, sensing them to be valuable despite never having worn one before. Then he joined the crowd of people, without knowing where they were hurrying to. Their destination turned out to be the main plaza, now aptly renamed 'Ebola Square.'

By then the local authorities had been stirred into action, roused by the continuous emergency calls transmitted by radios in the European quarter used only in dire emergencies. The virus was now roaming freely through the expat compound, circling in the bodies of milkmaids on their lucrative morning rounds and the blood of sewer-workers and plumbers come to mend a leak. The dutiful priest had also risked infection when he went to pray for the dead in the town's only church, and some of the more fervent locals had kissed his hands devoutly. But luckily his face was covered with several Riyyak Masks and his hands, always prey to his flock's kisses, were concealed beneath a thick pair of gloves.

Now, it seemed the whole area was in the know. It was as if they had been expecting just such an occurrence for some time. Everywhere precautions had been taken: gardens surrounded by barbed wire and abundant with home-grown vegetables; bread ovens run by the community's hardy women, capable of adapting to any circumstance or climate; and towers of long-life tinned goods transported from the inhabitants' home countries and stored in vast, spotless pantries.

Not a single foreigner would go hungry in Nzara, no matter how long Ebola endured. It was also highly unlikely that any would die.

But in times of crisis, terror is a law unto itself: it does not abide by class distinctions. It does not settle only on careworn faces but also on the smooth countenances of the wealthy and well protected.

The terror now reigning over the compound was no different to anywhere else: the same six letters forming the same word; the same taste in the mouth; the same scent in the nostrils; the same hysterical behaviour. The only difference was in the type of reflection it provoked. Among the wealthy classes, there was a more profound, philosophical type of rumination:

'What if this lasts for so long our prodigal children lose a vital year of education?'

'How quickly will our veins clot now we can't do our daily exercises?'

'What about our cholesterol?'

A shared angst pestered the compound's residents, joined in most homes by personal anxieties. A beautiful young woman, now housebound, suddenly realised she was no more than a dull housewife, no longer able to strut through the streets wafting her perfume and flicking her hair for a gaggle of gawping men to trail after. An old hunting fanatic faced the prospect of losing his rifle to rust now that its bullets could no longer reach either goat or gazelle. Then there were the stamp collectors whose search for lost letters had been abruptly halted when the post office suddenly became out of bounds.

The final fear was a rational one, grounded in science: that the virus gripping the region may not be the same as that discovered by Mushola, the Congolese doctor who was currently searching for a cure or vaccination. Perhaps this strain was different, a mutated version particular to the residents of Nzara.

Terror was also rife along the border, where fugitives from Congo had gathered. Among them was the great magician Jamadi Ahmed, begging for mercy from the border patrol who had neither heard nor read of such a concept in the instructions from their seniors. They were armed, unflinching and unafraid of Ebola, as per their orders. In a single spray of bullets, they shot down every donkey hauling frightened passengers towards the border. In a second round, they punctured the tires of jeeps and trucks, laden with the more affluent fugitives. As for those on foot, the only option was to take them down directly.

Despite the hysterical state he was in, Jamadi Ahmed

still had something of a military spirit. During his conscription in the Congolese Army he had picked up some of the soldiers' jargon, and much of it still lingered in his memory. He knew the soldiers were poor, and tethered by a long rope of obedience that lead back to some general, far out of harm's way in a luxurious office, or lounging on the Champs-Élysées watching Parisian women pass by from the Cardidor Café, or perhaps planning a military coup to replace one stale and reactionary regime with another just like it. Jamadi knew the respect normally afforded him as an elderly and well-known magician would be in short supply in the current circumstances. His fame amongst jailbirds and housewives, who invoked his name to scare their families into submission, was of little use to him amidst the jostling crowd, who were all begging for mercy. Jamadi's slogan, inscribed in red on his equipment case, was now rendered by Ebola a foolish scrawl that had entirely faded from people's minds. Jamadi knew he must not waste time swallowing ribbons and razors, nor pulling rabbits, doves or chickens from his case – it would only expose the poor animals to certain death. Instead, he approached a soldier with a silver beard. This was a sight uncommon in Africa, where silver beards grow only in old age, after an abundance of wisdom and memories have been accrued. Glancing at his shoulder, Jamadi found no indication of the soldier's rank, nor that of his colleagues. Although bemused by this battalion of apparent equals, he continued with his plan.

'Excuse me Sir!' he called out in his ordinary voice, the one he used at home, at the neighbours' place, or when buying cheese from the local shop – a tone altogether different from the resounding cries he used to excite the crowd in Zumbi Street when introducing a tired old routine.

'Excuse me Sir! I'd like to speak to the general in charge, if you please.' The soldier neither lowered his gun, nor glanced his way, but Jamadi heard his rough voice barking down from some way above, painfully reminding him of his own miserable stature. He wondered how he himself had come to be conscripted into the army all those years ago. How had they allowed someone as small as he was to battle their civil wars, knee-deep in blood and bones, until he learnt some magic tricks and was finally discharged from duty?

'We're all leaders of this battalion. We have the same rank but exchange positions every month. Now return to where you were.' The soldier's words were decisive and, if to be believed, it seemed the magician had stumbled across a fascinating case study within the military, certainly worth presenting to his communist comrades who, in their brief stints out of jail, had theorised everything – history, geography, theology – but never written a single word in praise or blame of the army. Jamadi resolved to address this, if they didn't all die of Ebola first. 'Look,' he would urge them, 'a whole battalion of soldiers and every month someone else is leader. Just look at that!'

However, for the time being Jamadi had taken more risks than he was comfortable with, and so he quietly backed away.

The frightened fugitives were scattered across the hard ground. Before them stretched a vast expanse of desiccated scrubland, eventually leading to a more appealing patch of green. From there they could observe the army barracks too – a disordered sprawl of buildings with rusting doors and grimy windows. The fugitives had food, drink and jugs of wine to while away the time and lessen their sense of impending doom. The men were also hoping some of the terrified women might turn out to be ex-prostitutes and – despite the climate of fear – would decide to resume their sordid business. No matter how strong or how real their terror, they had provisions and they had hope – they simply had to wait it out.

Unfortunately for these Congolese refugees, it did not matter how much they begged and pleaded. It did not even matter whether Jamadi and the others were eventually allowed to pass into southern Sudan. This would by no means signal the end of their ordeal. On the other side, the Sudanese border guards had been given special orders that nobody was to enter or leave, not only across the Congolese border, but also through the internal boundaries between Nzara and the other southern towns. And even if they did somehow manage to slip through those bounda-ries, their fate would still hang in the balance.

Meanwhile, in Nzara, the musical festivities were not going according to plan. Ruwadi Monti had nicknamed the concert 'The Show of Doom' after his thyroid had become almost fatally inflamed, appeased only when Darina reluctantly offered him some sedatives, feeling the first pangs of her menstrual cramps a week earlier than expected. One of the organisers had then disappeared for several hours, pursuing a group of street children selling face masks. He returned with twenty masks and handed them out. While wandering around he had also bumped into James Riyyak, who was trawling the danger zone in his jeep and had forsaken masks for sheer good luck. The young man urged Riyyak to design some musicians' gloves and a protective head covering suitable for a bushy head of hair and, if possible, to make some cotton shoes in a size forty-eight.

The reason, he explained, was that he was currently playing host to a musician more demanding and more of a nuisance than any other he had ever encountered.

In truth, Ruwadi's outburst had nothing to do with having a melodramatic temperament; it was simply the effect of the terrible thyroxine hormone wreaking havoc in every cell of his body. He had not abandoned the idea of leaving his current hovel for a more secure building designed to make the sound of an ant's movements audible. In such terrifying times, Ruwadi lost the ability to distinguish between the precautions necessary for deterring thieves and those needed to block out an invisible threat dancing gleefully all around. Finally, when the organisers realised that playing deaf was of no use and that the profits from the concert had become completely valueless, since everything in the town had lost its value, they moved Ruwadi to another house, belonging to an Arab tradesman. The man in question did not dispute their proposed rate, given everything happening in the city. As for the Imperial Leather, there was none to be found in the markets, and the only shampoo available was a cheap variety that Ruwadi had had to reluctantly accept.

Riyyak promised to deliver the gloves and the head covering as soon as possible, but informed them that he didn't have any cotton shoes among his old collection, or the items produced since Ebola. It would not be possible for him to design anything new, either, since his mental energy had been spent in full on producing the masks. Besides, even if he were to think something up, there simply wasn't the machinery to make it.

ELEVEN

By the time Lewis came to Ebola Square the dead and the half dead were piled high, while the living bustled back and forth, their masks covering their faces as they assisted the over-burdened Doctor Luther, who had been working flat out for several days. His helpers were some of the people Ebola had spared, who brought with them their own experience of being at death's door, plus an understanding of what it was like to return to life's embrace. This meant they could instruct the sick on what their death would be like, should that be their fate and, if not, what they would experience upon regaining life. Besides this, the helpers were also skilled in detecting a false deathbed awakening. Carefully monitoring the invalids as they awoke, they analysed their speech and facial expressions, and upon discovering a false awakening, they would immediately break into hysterical ululations.

A rumour had recently spread through the square that news of the epidemic had finally reached the necessary people, and teams of specialists would shortly be arriving by helicopter from Juba and Khartoum, as well as from wealthy foreign nations. It was agreed that all those alive to witness the great breakthrough should never forget those who had sacrificed their lives along the way.

Just as Lewis arrived in the square, however, a brawl broke out. Several witnesses were insisting the mass burial site did not contain only the dead. Voices had been heard screaming desperately from the pit for help, but nobody had had the courage to answer them. As far as Doctor Luther was concerned, his obligations were limited to saving the lives of those in front of him. He would not be heading into a filthy pit, not even to rescue living beings crying for help. In any case, Ebola had most likely taken them back into its frenzied clutches, so even if they were rescued, they would probably die shortly afterwards.

As Luther and his volunteers laboured on, the witnesses continued to cause a stir, invoking the word 'humanity' within a long string of vitriolic abuse. It was perhaps the first time in its history that the term – respected and revered the world over – had been so sullied.

Lewis looked on attentively. He knew anyone who still had their wits about them would be able to recognise him: not by his face, which was covered with a Riyyak Mask, but by the dirty hospital gown exposing his furry bottom-half. Lewis, in turn, was able to recognise many of the crowd, both the sick and the volunteers. He spotted his neighbour, who had once made a living by selling the cheese she made from her own cows' milk. During her deathbed awakening she cursed the world in its entirety, revealing that she had once seen Sultan Kojak's private parts when he had deliberately exposed himself to her whilst buying milk. The Sultan was one of the city's most eminent and respected figures. Nobody – not even his adversaries or enemies – would have imagined someone had seen his privates, not even one of his ten wives.

Lewis also recognised a colleague from the factory who happened to have been nominated for the forthcoming Man of the Year award. The man had revived some time before Lewis's arrival, however, and had already undergone his awakening and passed away. He was shortly to be taken to the mass grave, to join the rest of the dead.

Among other familiar faces was that of the bus driver who had brought Lewis from Kinshasa, and the apothecary Mansour, who was well known to the local men for having illegitimately fathered a large number of southern Sudan's children. This was the very same Mansour who had given Tina her fertility medicines, not missing the opportunity to touch her up in the process. Now it was apparent that he had stumbled, once again, into one of the city's iniquitous dens where he had fumbled with an infected woman.

Despite his fears, nobody so much as gestured in Lewis's direction to accuse him of bringing the disease to the town or of being its partner in crime. He heard not a single word of reproach. Then, when one of the volunteers asked him to come and help – since he had been the first to die and return to life with all his mental faculties intact – it suddenly dawned on Lewis that he had, in fact, survived. At that moment, Lewis felt the coffee bean wine drain from his head all in one go, as if the busy square had purged it from him.

'Where's Tina?' Lewis cried, running deeper into the chaos that was spreading steadily across the town, despite the busy hands working to keep it at bay. Lewis couldn't spot Tina anywhere. His gaze settled on one woman after another but none were Tina – all were either too fat or too ugly.

Lewis was told to look in the mass grave. Tina was most likely there, dead or alive. He had heard about the grave earlier on, from the brawling crowd, but his intoxicated state at that time had prevented him from properly digesting the information. Besides, Lewis didn't believe it was possible for any woman – least of all his wife – to go a whole day without food. And so, rather than going to investigate as he should have done, Lewis dashed home, rejoicing in his new lease of life and resolving to dedicate it to continued adultery.

Arriving at the house he found the door was open. There were still visible traces of Tina's tearful collapse in front of Anami. On the floor, the dirty dish water had dried and grass had sprouted in its place. The entrance was now free of stones, and the mattress was covered with their scarlet nuptial sheets. Several bags of Angelica, Monk's Pepper and Maca stood on a wooden table near the bed, and on the dressing table, along with Tina's cracked mirror, was a tub of face powder, a pot of face cream and a lipstick.

At the sight of this, all inclination to be unfaithful abandoned Lewis. He was convulsed by memories in the most unexpected way. Images from the past flashed before his eyes: the successes and the failures, the precious moments and the frivolous, his idiocies and his moments of insight. Lewis remembered each of the sixteen girls he had pursued as a youth. Of the sixteen, one (who happened to be partially-sighted) had initially responded to his attentions, but even she had abandoned him soon afterwards. Lewis remembered how he had resolved to marry the first girl he saw smiling in the street, and how he had spotted Tina dressed in her mother's threadbare trousers with a smile on her face. He recalled the colic and the fever, the nights when he'd behaved like a saint, and the others when he'd committed the most unforgivable outrages.

When Lewis was a youth, people had fallen into one of two categories: huntsmen and rebels. The first charged into the jungles, delighting in the mysteries that lay among the trees. The second battled tirelessly against the government, rejecting its unjust constitutions and accomplishing great acts of heroism to be preserved in legend. Lewis, meanwhile, was a lowly servant, running back and forth from the market for his scornful French masters, and wiping their children's dirty backsides. At best, he was permitted to gaze in awe at the paintings by Manet and Giovanni that hung on their walls. Everything Tina's nosy neighbour had imagined about Lewis was unfortunately true. His mother really had thrown him into rubbish dumps and his brothers really were ruthless thieves who'd left for Khartoum many years ago after hearing of the riches to be had there.

That morning, Lewis wept bitterly for his whole wretched life, from his first newborn cry, to that present moment as he lay sprawled on the scarlet sheets covering the ancient wooden bed. He realised Tina had not been so bad after all, her mother Ashoul hadn't really despised him, and Uncle Majouk was nothing but a second-rate performer who took to atheism to overcome his limitations but never succeeded in doing so. He realised Anami had, after all, deserved to be factory foreman, because he was creative and skilful and dedicated to his work. And James Riyyak deserved to die. He had never treated anyone fairly in his life and the precious war he'd waged in the jungle was nothing but a mad struggle for power – had he been victorious and gained the control he had ardently desired, nobody would have escaped his shackles.

Again, Lewis found himself overtaken by murderous imaginings. If only he had the strength to make them a reality, to kill Riyyak and burn his factory to the ground before Ebola got there first. But such hopes were futile. Ebola alone was conversant in the language of death.

Lewis was brought back to his senses by the sound of the door creaking open, announcing the arrival of a visitor. Under less unusual circumstances, this would not have been so surprising. Indeed, Lewis would have expected several beasts to be slaughtered in celebration of his recovery, and all sorts of visitors to descend on the house.

TWELVE

There was no doubt about it. James Riyyak was mad.

This had been the deadly Ebola's impression of him from the very first moment it hovered in his vicinity, and yet the virus had still been unable to strike him down.

In fact the whole town had held this same impression of Riyyak, ever since the days of the rebellion, including his wife before she left him for a Kenyan lorry driver. And now Lewis Nawa thought the same as he stood face to face with Riyyak, who had barged into his house, driving every other thought from his mind.

Rather surprisingly, however, Riyyak seemed neither malicious nor aggressive. On the contrary, he was rather pleasant and completely calm, with a jovial expression on his face that Lewis had never seen him show before.

As Ebola continued to kill and wreak havoc, depriving wives of their husbands, neighbours of their neighbours, children of their parents and lovers of their loved ones, James Riyyak began to doubt his long-standing reputation as a lucky devil. Son of a whore, child of the backwaters, offspring of a stray – these all seemed closer to the truth. Deep down, Riyyak acknowledged that the tree his unlucky aircraft had plummeted into was a strong one, bound to catch the plane, and that the rat poison his wife had marinated the gazelle meat with was not really so toxic and, at any rate, would have been evident from the very first bite. As for the Molotov cocktail in the hands of that idiotic soldier, it hadn't really required much skill to dispose of it.

That morning Riyyak had gone to the factory as usual. Ever since he'd made peace with the authorities, the place had been his life. He headed for his office and picked up the register where his employees recorded their arrivals (always far earlier than the reality) but there was not a single name. Riyyak hurried to the factory floor, hoping to hear the usual roar of machinery: nothing. The machines were all deadly silent, and it even seemed like a few stray cats had clambered into them and soiled the unfinished garments hanging inside. Despite his fury, the possibility of a strike did not occur to Riyyak, although it was the most obvious conclusion at such a time, when even the coming of judgement day seemed plausible. Having promised special gloves and a protective head covering to the concert organisers – and been paid in advance – he needed to begin production right away.

At that point, Riyyak's gaze suddenly fell on the old machine that Lewis Nawa had operated for so many years. He had been on the verge of getting rid of it and replacing it with the new one that was still lurking in a corner of the room. The new machine had erased Lewis's name from the register even before the virus had taken him, but when Ebola struck the city, Riyyak's plans for its inauguration were scuppered.

The old machine was still in its place, looking much the same as the others in service. Right up until the last time Lewis had operated it, before travelling to Kinshasa, the machine had produced shirts, trousers and simple yet elegant shawls, without any problem.

Riyyak approached the silent machine and gave a firm military salute, addressing it as 'General.' Twitching nervously, he vowed that it would remain where it was forevermore, and that it would return to work immediately, with Lewis at the helm. After making these exaggerated promises, Riyyak went to operate one of the newer machines. Tense and frustrated, he worked there for an hour until he'd finally finished the musician's gloves. Then he put them in a paper bag bearing the factory's logo and headed into the streets of Nzara. He did not turn to even glance at the scenes of suffering filling the streets. Riyyak had already heard of the death of Anami Okiyano and many other workers, all of whom had represented the very life force of the factory. Anami had apparently exhibited the most vicious of deathbed awakenings, entirely dedicated to exposing his boss. He had enumerated every single bad thing about James Riyyak without touching on any of the good, as if there wasn't an ounce of benevolence in him − as if he had not brought a fully operational and productive factory to an immobile town and provided wages to its workers. Riyyak had learnt that in the few minutes before his death Anami had also spoken, with confidence and clarity, of an affair he had had with a woman married to a vicious man. He had described the woman naked, the way she looked in her resplendent necklaces as she combed her hair, and how she would exfoliate her feet with a rough stone and scrape the fungal skin out from between her toes. Okiyano did not actually state that the woman was

Riyyak's wife Hannah, but the description was more than sufficient for him to realise.

'That stupid bimbo! She'd go with any Kenyan who'd take her,' Riyyak muttered to himself bitterly.

Riyyak had often thought about pursuing Hannah to the Nairobi den she had holed up in after running away with her Kenyan lorry driver, who had never reappeared in Nzara since. Riyyak had considered sending a band of skilled assassins to reduce Hannah to a bloody pulp; he had even started to scout seriously for such merciless types. Luckily, Nzara had never been home to a hit man, someone prepared to kill without any personal ill-will. From the days of the rebellion, Riyyak knew men with a taste for blood, yet all refused his proposal once he had divulged the details.

'There are several steps we'd need to take for this to work,' replied each of the men he had approached. 'Firstly, we'd have to take her back to Nzara and she'd have to live with you so you could get an official divorce. Then we'd have to marry her officially and let her flee with the Kenyan guy again, so we could kill her as a personal vendetta.'

Hannah's flight was no laughing matter. By Riyyak's own assessment – according to the strict dictates of his masculinity – it was very serious indeed. He was, after all, a former rebel leader, hounded by the authorities in his day, his name appearing in countless speeches by successive ministers at the loathsome Ministry of Defence. The prime minister had even mentioned his name once, in a speech to celebrate Flag Day in El Fasher, in the northwest of the country. Riyyak had heard it himself on the radio as he was lying low in the jungle. Even by his current standards – as one of the few successful businessmen in those far-flung towns, recognised by the national government for having helped the country's economic revival – it was a serious matter.

In Ebola Square, the air quivered with anxiety and echoed with groans of pain, while the ground was covered in bodies, most of them more dead than alive. Riyyak took out a face mask he had designed especially for himself, assembled from a combination of cotton and plastic. Very carefully, he tied it to his face, no longer willing to rely on luck alone. He then began asking after Lewis, the man who had brought the disease to Nzara and then survived it. Those who had noticed Lewis's bare lower half as he rummaged through the female corpses in search of his wife informed Riyyak that Lewis had been there about an hour ago. At that point one of Riyyak's employees – who hadn't been playing truant on purpose, but was genuinely absent due to sickness – informed him that, whilst he had nothing against Riyyak, it would be in the boss's best interests to keep a safe distance and a level head at the time of his deathbed awakening, since the example demonstrated by Anami Okiyano seemed to be a general trend for Riyyak's workforce. In truth, Riyyak did not particularly resent Anami Okiyano, despite everything he had learnt – even after Anami's elaborate revelations concerning his wife. Indeed, if he were to come back to life, Riyyak would reemploy him without hesitation.

Riyyak drove his jeep to the death pit. Flames spilled from the mouth of the pit and the stench of rotting corpses filled the air, along with the piercing cries of those within who refused to surrender to their fate. Riyyak quickly sped off in the direction of the market. He knew that Lewis would be hungry and penniless, and was certain he could be bought for the price of a meal. In the market there were faint signs of life. Rumours that an important rescue operation was imminent had spread through the city, encouraging some of the tradesmen to get business going again, having been glued to their stations in silence for some time now. They had begun sprinkling water in front of their stalls to create some humidity in the dry climate, and were now shaking the dust from their goods. They began to warm up their voices too, a necessity after several days' silence. They practised the usual market cries, the sort heard the world over, lauding the goods on sale and denying their slightest imperfection.

Riyyak watched the vendors closely, observing their burgeoning activity. To his delight he noticed they were wearing his masks. He bought a few luxuries from some of the stalls, in aid of what he called the beginning of 'serious resistance' against Ebola. Then he purchased some cheap food, climbed back into his car and headed to Lewis's house, almost certain he would find him there, drunk and hopeless as always.

In his anxious state Riyyak had promised the old machine it would work again, and work it must.

On a stool in the small sitting room of Lewis's house, Riyyak sat with his legs outstretched. The strain of driving the jeep around town touting his masks several times a day for the last few days, combined with his advancing age, had left him exhausted. His voice was also tired out from delivering sales pitches and coming up with meanings for the random symbols on the masks. He was thus hoping Lewis would respond to his requests without needing too much persuasion, and without him having to resort to the battle talk of revolution he now only used in moments of grave urgency. Without uttering a word, Riyyak passed Lewis a greasy paper bag. The smell of onion and garlic wafted into the air and Lewis snatched the bag, ripped it open and scoffed down what was a rather unusual meal, not for its taste or because of Ebola, but because it came offered by a hand so unaccustomed to giving.

Lewis was not the sharpest of men. Indeed, he was usually oblivious to whatever was happening around him, and generally unable to distinguish clearly between good and bad, but even he could see that this meal had not been given out of charity.

'Yes, Captain?' Lewis muttered through the last mouthful; he was reluctant to swallow it, even though he had already chewed it into an easily digestible pulp. His mouth was smeared with grease, but his head much clearer after the sudden rush of sugar in his bloodstream. The nurse's biscuits had not been nearly sufficient to regulate the blood sugar level of someone so ravenous.

Lewis had not chosen the word 'Captain' at random; it was the title all the workers were made to use, amidst the racket of the machines. Even in his mind, when he imagined himself murdering Riyyak, Lewis had thought of him as 'Captain.' None of the workers in Riyyak's factory were capable of speaking to him face to face without using this term, which clearly separated the shepherd from his sheep. Over the years, however, the workers had learnt how to pronounce the word with an undetectable spite, an entirely unapparent rage bubbling inside. They could speak it from the tip of the tongue, and make it sound as if it were coming from some deep, earnest place within. Anami Okiyano, above all, was master of insulting Riyyak in such a way, just as though he was praising him.

'Yes, Captain.' In his state of resentful satisfaction, Lewis attempted to utter the word out of malice, but he could not.

There he was, alone before the boss. Not even Tina was there to assist him with her womanly charm and cunning, should Riyyak sense his distain.

'Listen Lewis, I want you to come back to work right away. We'll work together, you and I, until the great rescue gets here. You'll soon see for yourself I don't really own a man-eating wolf or drink a cup of blood before bed every night. You'll see me sleeping, and you'll smell my farts, because we'll be living together at the factory. We'll be fully dedicated to our cause, even when we wake up in the night needing a piss. We will defeat Ebola! Come on, Lewis! Get up!'

It seemed Riyyak was quite aware of the rumours that had circulated widely about him among the factory workers and their relatives. In actual fact, he had only just learned of them the day before from the wife of an employee who, during her deathbed awakening, had repeated verbatim what she had heard her husband say.

Lewis hesitated, filled with fear, even though the Captain's eyes seemed calm and his tone was not commanding, despite those final words being uttered in the imperative. He had no idea how to respond. James Riyyak, with his companionable words and his hot edible offering, had turned Lewis's thoughts from murder to a sense of indebtedness. If he wasn't careful, he might end up being completely under Riyyak's thumb, and he certainly didn't want that.

THIRTEEN

The people were in a state of mindless frenzy. This was not – in most cases – down to stupidity. The cause was fear. It was this very terror that presented a golden opportunity for the artists of the region to attract a large audience desperately in need of distraction, and a movement began to form that would soon earn the title 'Fight Fear with Art.'

This very same idea had arisen in the minds of both Jamadi Ahmed and Ruwadi Monti, upon finding themselves hopelessly ensnared by Ebola. From Jamadi's position at the border, where he sat with his props – animate and inanimate – alongside hundreds of other terrified refugees, it seemed a straightforward task. For the guitarist Ruwadi Monti, it was far from simple. By this point, Ruwadi was wearing several Riyyak Masks, a pair of coarse gloves entirely unsuitable for his slender fingers, and some cotton sandals Darina had sewn by hand with a blunt needle one of the organisers had brought from home. Hopefully these accessories would curtail the hysterical screaming fits she feared might become a permanent habit of Ruwadi's, even after the end of their current predicament, should they emerge from it intact.

A light mist hung in the air that morning, along with the scent of approaching rain, although none materialised. By now the borders were in a gloomy limbo, and the soldiers continued to rotate their positions, still not letting on whether their joint leadership was for real or not. While one group returned to the nearby barracks to rest, wash and copulate with their wives – should they be married – the others would head back to the borders for a proper rest, eating and drinking, combing their beards and polishing their heavy boots, ever ready to explode in a rage at the slightest disturbance.

The previous day, hundreds of newcomers had arrived from Kinshasa, multiplying the swarming masses, and sadly bringing no news to confirm the government's alleged victory over the virus. Some attributed this lack of development to the fact that containing a virus is a tricky business, requiring much planning and preparation before a strategy can be implemented, and so they had decided to flee while waiting. The cynics among them denied the existence of any such strategy, and insisted there was therefore nothing to wait for.

'If the government was really serious about everything it announced then I'd still have my eye!' cried a former military fireman who'd lost one eye in an enormous blaze. During the slow march of terror that day, it was this man's words that struck the crowd as the most eloquent and symbolic commentary on the situation.

Jamadi Ahmed had always had a keen interest in anyone or anything with bizarre talents or an odd appearance that might contribute to his magic show. Despite encountering many potential candidates in his long career, however, he'd never taken any of them on. He had failed to appreciate the talents of a performing ewe that had frolicked before his very eyes while imitating the bellow of an ox. Nor had he embraced the giant, non-venomous snake offered to him by an Indian traveller he'd met in Kinshasa. The Indian had asked a modest three francs for the snake, yet Jamadi declined, allowing someone else to snap up the deal. Then there was a young country girl, Talinka, who could apparently consume glass as though it were a tasty treat. Jamadi had travelled to the girl's home, observed her talents and taken several photographs, only to leave her for another less experienced magician to make a small fortune from. Finally, there was Jamadi's own nephew, who had mastered the art of the skipping rope at a young age, and could easily have become a circus star. Jamadi had undervalued the boy's talents entirely and, eventually, he moved to Canada and became a pole-vault champion.

There were many noteworthy oddballs amongst the current crowd of fugitives, some whose talents were already well honed and others still a little rough around the edges. It was impossible to ascertain whether their blood was free from Ebola's boisterous attentions, but the past few days there had been no deaths, and no spluttering coughs or haemorrhaging skin – all promising signs that the theatre of resistance was clean.

Of course, Jamadi paid no attention to the vegetable sellers, plumbers, car mechanics or bakers – nor even to the popular Congolese poets, or the folk musicians who had shamefully abandoned their instruments when fleeing the city, ruining their chances of proving their celebrity. None of these people embodied the kind of talent Jamadi was looking for.

Soon, however, the magician came across two young women who proved very keen to feature in the 'Fight Fear with Art' programme. Isabella had been a student at the High School for the Arts in Kinshasa before fleeing the city with her mother and siblings, and had been due to sing at a charity benefit, having composed her very own song, which she performed with great gusto. The spread of the disease in her country had unfortunately quenched her hopes, however, as the event was abruptly cancelled. Mariam, meanwhile, had no interest in the arts, nor any connection to them. She was determined to work in politics, not by clawing her way up the ranks of a defunct old party, but by establishing her own. It would be called the 'Sun Party' and would perennially stand in opposition. In Mariam's country, the ephemeral song of democracy did not play; there were no fair elections to bring governments to power and shun them should they fail. Rather, there were military men. Military men who ruled, military men who rebelled, and military men plotting for yet another coup.

In his new cabaret show, put together under the pressure of great terror, Jamadi Ahmed had decided that the two girls should suddenly disappear from sight and then reappear behind the audience, or under their feet, or maybe even above their heads. The exact results of such a stunt were unpredictable and, back in the safety of Zumbi Street, Jamadi had always been too afraid to try it. He had, however, given the trick a go the day he arrived at the borders, attempting to make the hard-nosed soldiers disappear. Nobody had vanished though. Jamadi decided he probably hadn't been concentrating hard enough, or the guards had been issued with talismans of some sort to protect themselves from such spells. Without further reflection, he thus busied himself with his new show, ignoring the chaos around him and the fearful hypothesising over what was to come.

A new whisper had begun to circulate: that the authorities were planning to drop a one-tonne petrol bomb on the people so as to restore order.

'How exactly do you expect us to fight this fear with art?'

'How do you expect us to sing and clap to dances and magic tricks? How do you expect us to gasp and cheer when we don't know what's to become of us? How? How? How?'

Many were the questions the crowd posed, designed to cut Jamadi to the quick. What's more, amongst all the negativity, not a single man or woman was heard to shout, 'Can it be? The great magician Jamadi Ahmed standing before our very eyes!'

Under normal circumstances, Jamadi had no need for such cries of admiration, which neither kept him in food nor held death at bay. Right then, however, he felt a little encouragement might aid his concentration. He had considered whispering in the ear of the old crone who had once adored him, egging her on to a scream of amazement. She seemed less than interested, however, crouching on the ground eating a piece of stale bread, and eventually Jamadi thought better of it. Then he thought of bribing one of the young shaven-headed men to give an admiring cry, but soon decided against that too. Instead, he began taking his props from his case, starting the show with some familiar old tricks: breathing from the scalp, turning a dove into a rabbit, turning a rabbit into a chicken, swallowing razor blades and bringing them back up in a ribbon. Nobody seemed to have noticed him, and so he began racing through his acts at a manic pace, desperately hoping for someone to applaud, and even resolving to break his own non-handshaking rule if anyone should present themselves. But nobody did . . .

The fear was not being fought with art, but with an additional dose of fear. Not even the two girls, Isabella and Mariam, seemed particularly interested in the campaign. Instead they avoided Jamadi's gaze and ignored his instructions, running away from the crowd and starting a game of hopscotch in an attempt to fight the fear with frolicking.

In the end even Jamadi decided to give in to his fear, as everyone else had done. He packed up his equipment, desperately wishing his whole routine would die a swift death so he could finally be free, a magician no more.

Ruwadi Monti was in no better state. But he had given up on his fits of anxiety and had stopped wasting his time hanging around the streets. The protective gloves had also been abandoned, and replaced with large doses of liver-damaging thyroid medication. Had he not given up drinking years ago, he would have happily added a strong beverage to the mix.

'Darina, friends . . . Let's fight this fear with art! Are you with me?'

But the organisers were decidedly not with Ruwadi. Time and again they had told him that his fame had little meaning in the midst of the prevailing crisis, and that all he could do was wait and see if the star of his celebrity would eventually shine out again once the night was not so clouded by tragedy.

They did not specify how long the wait would be (one, two, ten days?), having neither Ebola's sense of precision, nor an astrologer's ability to predict the future.

Darina was terrified. It was as though she had become two different people: the first was a pretty girl, always attentive to her looks, who was often to be found gazing in the mirror and knew a thing or two about glossy hair and provocative clothing. Like all girls of her generation, this Darina dreamed of knights on horseback and happy endings and certainly would not be taking Ruwadi's side. But the other Darina, Darina the human walking stick, plucked from the streets by Ruwadi, raised in his own home and taken with him wherever he went, this Darina would be with him for sure.

She was truly torn. What's more, only a week before travelling to Nzara, Darina had met a man who had appeared to value her as a woman rather than a walking stick. She had been dining with Ruwadi in a posh restaurant they went to on occasion. Even in restaurants, Darina was Ruwadi's aide, steadying his soup as it wobbled in his hands, helping him sort the potatoes from the meat, and telling him a dirty joke or two to ensure the dinner passed without incident. Yet, deep in her heart – one no different to any other, despite being that of a foundling – Darina fostered her own ambitions. She had long wished for a real father with a real name, and a real mother to nag her when she slouched and pull her dress over her knees when they were in company. But Darina knew she was a nobody without having to ask. At least Ruwadi posed no threat to her maidenhood. For one thing, he could not see her, and besides he was married to his ancient guitar, having pledged it his loyalty in sickness and in health with all the pomp and ceremony of a strict catholic service. After separating from his last wife, Ruwadi had announced that his decision was irrevocable and that, if a rival to his guitar ever entered the house, he would spurn her advances and retreat into the instrument's embrace.

The man in the restaurant had flashed Darina a broad smile, then come over to join their table. Badidi, a successful tennis player, was well known – possibly even more so than Ruwadi. He was also a bachelor, and not bad looking either. Badidi's mother had passed away two years before that, triggering a nervous breakdown from which he had only recently recovered. Friends and acquaintances were now urging him to get married, telling him he needed his mother or, at the least, a girl who resembled her.

The Needle was, of course, thrilled to have another celebrity at the table. He allotted him a small portion of his dining hour, since he had no other time available. Intuitively, Ruwadi could tell the man was wearing sports gear, and the chain rattling around his neck was definitely not 24-carat gold. He could also sense that the warmth he exhibited was intended only for Darina.

There are few other details to the story. Darina fell for the tennis player, and was convinced he had fallen for her too. The excessive confidence she held in her own pretty face, captivating speech and perfect figure had prevented her from noticing that the sportsman was rather distracted during the hour they spent together. Badidi had been lost in thoughts of his late mother, attempting to compare her with the woman before him, without coming to any conclusion about how similar they were.

And now, Ruwadi was calling for her once more: 'Darina! Friends! Let us fight side by side. Let's fight this fear with art! Let's take music to the diseased streets.'

There was not so much as a murmur of response. The organisers were busy calculating the losses they would make from cancelling their next six concerts, where other popular musicians had been scheduled to perform. The musicians had been invited from Kenya, Uganda, the Ivory Coast and Khartoum. Osman Hussein, the region's greatest singer, was even on the list, chosen with the Arab audience in mind. The Arabs were by no means a minority in the area and, given their relative affluence, would be prepared to pay double just to hear him sing 'Forgive Me Baby.' Darina, meanwhile, was daydreaming of her tennis player, writing a letter to him in her heart without knowing if he would ever get to read it: *My love . . . Wait for me in the same restaurant . . . This disaster will soon be over and I will return.*

By then, Ruwadi had realised he would have to work alone. He promised himself that if he survived he would never perform in Nzara again, nor any other place for that matter. Never again. He would marry Darina off to one of the thuggish Dambtalou clan, should any of them happen to be out of prison and free from Ebola. Leaning heavily on his chair, Ruwadi rose, clutching his guitar in his right hand and feeling his way with his left. His nose filled with the stench of the main road. He clung to his ancient guitar and took several steps before stumbling on a metal sheet leaning against one of the walls. The organisers had finished calculating their losses and were observing his hesitant progress. Darina had not yet finished her love letter, but got up anyway. She would follow him down the street, and accept whatever consequences came of it.

The dead had no use for a famous and talented musician, the half dead were more concerned with finding a doctor or vaccine, and the healthy were still so overcome with terror that art had no chance against it.

Art was for art's sake. That was the rule in those critical days. Fear could only be fought with greater fear. In the streets, Ruwadi strummed his guitar, playing a number of the rallying military marches taught in Congolese schools to instil nationalist sentiments. But not a single person stopped to listen. The people passing by seemed utterly oblivious, so Ruwadi switched from military marches to desperate love songs, and got no better response. He grew tired, and so did Darina and the concert organisers, who were sulking in the background. Just as it had done at the borders, fear defeated art in the streets and alleys of Nzara.

And so it seemed nothing could fight fear quite as well as greater fear did. Art and beauty had no sway in the time of Ebola. On the way back to their luxurious residence, Ruwadi looked as if he were about to say something, but no words came.

FOURTEEN

Lewis had betrayed his loved ones, propelled to Kinshasa by his own lust, only to bring back a virus that would kill those around him and leave him alive to remember them, ever more vaguely. Things could not get worse.

There he was, forcing down his food and belching miserably as he worked. Entirely against his will, he was going to revive that factory which had never done anything of the sort for him, even in his hour of greatest need. Things really could not get worse.

With a cheerful expression, Riyyak had requested Lewis return to work immediately. Yet his appeal – posited in the most gentle of tones – remained unanswered as Lewis sat muttering to himself.

Lewis's poor brain was overcome with confusion. Riyyak, the ex-rebel, on the other hand, was calm and composed enough to run a business even in those most horrific of circumstances. How did he manage it? How could he be so quick to exploit the terror, unafraid of contagion and untroubled by his conscience?

Lewis had no answers to his own questions. He was also forced to admit that he too had failed to heed his conscience when he had the chance, both after his deathbed awakening, and again during that second dawning of awareness. He lay sprawled on the scarlet sheets, the house's memories weighing down on him, memories with no power to bring back those already lost. Yet there he was, questioning Riyyak's moral compass, this man who had clearly stated, on dozens of occasions, and even when not prompted, that he would continue to squeeze the most out of life until his very last breath – and that nothing mattered beyond that.

What's more, Lewis was now indebted to Riyyak because of the meal he had brought round to him. It probably wasn't worth much, and Lewis knew he could have bartered for food in the market and owed the Arab traders something instead. Or he could probably have broken into one of the padlocked shops to steal some bread and tins, and become indebted to his own courageous banditry. If forced to, he could even have earned a mouthful sweeping a dirty terrace for the ex-pats, or wiping the bottoms of a few French brats. Or he could have offered his precious services in the fight against Ebola. Usually, the authorities were happy to feed anyone still willing to eat after witnessing so much death.

Lewis sat muttering to himself, trying fruitlessly to revive his earlier murderous daydreams. When Riyyak repeated his request it was no longer a gentle plea, delivered in casual terms as he reclined on the old sofa. This time it was a command, without any hint of gratitude. Riyyak got to his feet, put on his mask and gloves and grabbed Lewis by the hand, dragging him into the next room where the last traces of Tina Azacouri lingered. The scent of incense hung in the air, a remnant of the couple's recent night of passion. Riyyak threw Lewis onto the creaky bed, pulling some grey overalls from the wardrobe. He stripped him of the dirty hospital gown and dressed him in his work clothes, pretending not to notice the absolutely tragic state of his shrivelled genitals. The whole process was accomplished with the astonishing speed Riyyak was famous for, the same speed with which he had confronted danger upon danger during the rebellion, and whipped up his very own line of Riyyak Masks during the early days of the epidemic.

Lewis suddenly found himself in Riyyak's jeep, unhappily prevented by the circumstances from enjoying what was, without doubt, the smoothest ride of his life, and the plushest, most velvety seat he had ever sat upon. By this point the silent factory was under occupation by a pack of stray cats, and a few dogs who were trying to drive them out, just to pass the time. Riyyak parked Lewis in front of the old machine that, thanks to the disease and subsequent scarcity of workers, had recently been promoted to the rank of General. Then he ordered Lewis to begin working.

'What am I working on, Captain?' Lewis asked, innocently enough, but with the slightest suggestion of a snarl on the final word.

'What you were working on before,' Riyyak answered.

'I can't, Captain,' Lewis responded, the growl in his voice making it quite clear this time that by 'Captain' he meant 'Go to hell.'

'It's not the right time to be making things. I'm in mourning for Tina. The whole city's in mourning.'

But Riyyak would not go to hell, or anywhere other than his factory, for that matter. His rebel tendencies – forsaken for many years – had started to show themselves once more, and he slunk cautiously over to the factory door, which stood ajar. After glancing into the street, he shut the door softly before heading to his office. He returned carrying an unlicensed machine gun which had been stowed away in a wooden drawer in one of the cupboards. He loaded the gun and positioned it on his shoulder, standing stock still as the old machine rattled back into life. With increasing delight he observed Lewis's shaking knees, and watched as he poked a dry tongue out of his mouth, attempting to moisten his quivering lips.

At that moment, Riyyak had an unsettling thought: who were they making things for? In its bartering with death, the town had almost stripped down to its underwear, and all trade routes to neighbouring countries had been shut off. Yet, with the same optimism that had led him to believe his assaults against the government would end in a satisfactory settlement – a belief which proved true when he was granted a substantial sum of money and a large plot of land on which he had built that very factory – Riyyak was confident the epidemic would die down and life would improve. As for the issue of his wife, hiding somewhere in Kenya with that sissy lorry driver, that wasn't really a problem. One day, he would find her, and when he did, he'd disfigure her so badly no one would ever want to kidnap her again. Besides this, Riyyak took the most comfort in the fact that Hannah had never borne him a child and he was thus forever relieved of the burden of consideration for his descendants.

The General was turning slowly, pumping out thick smoke and spitting bits of coagulated excrement deposited by the feral cats. Threads of various colours – blues, reds, purples – spun together, forming shirts, scarves and shawls that provided warmth and a certain simple elegance. Despite his unstoppable trembling, Lewis remained glued to his seat. He was a prisoner, for no crime other than not being dead. Later, he discovered the plain pyjamas Riyyak had made him from leftover cotton, along with a basic toothbrush and a lousy beard-trimmer Riyyak had bought him. Riyyak had also dumped a cloth mattress in the corner that Lewis was permitted to rest on at specified times.

For the first time since his recovery, Lewis also began to wish he had not survived after all. In comparison to his current joyless existence, death seemed immensely preferable.

Strangely enough, Ebola was not in the two men's vicinity at that particular moment. Lewis, it seemed, had been abandoned by the virus after it had delivered its message in the most violent of manners. Riyyak, meanwhile, appeared to be of little interest to it. Or perhaps Ebola was saving him for the show-stopping death he deserved. In an unambitious backwater such as Nzara, the demise of a figure such as James Riyyak would certainly raise the people's downcast spirits. His deathbed awakening would be no ordinary, ugly, repetitive confession of love affairs, either: his would bring a little more complexity, what with his secret life in the jungle, his business affairs, and his volatile relationship with the authorities.

In Ebola Square, work continued. Doctor Luther, who had not yet been struck down, despite wallowing in the mire for hours on end, declared there was no more medication to treat the victims' restricted blood flow, no painkillers for their headaches and fevers and no gauze left for their wounds. There was no one to give blood either and, even if there had been, there was no way of testing their blood type or knowing whether they were already infected with the virus. Following this the doctor announced in a composed and sober tone that his colleague, Nasraddin Akwi, had died that morning, having valiantly battled the epidemic. He would not be flung in the communal grave with the other victims, even if it was a communal disease that had killed him. No, the doctor would be buried in a manner befitting his reputation.

Nobody knew what had transpired during Doctor Akwi's deathbed awakening, and, even if he had known, Dr Luther would never have made it public.

Meanwhile, at the border, some new developments had occurred. It seemed Riyyak's idea to turn catastrophe into profit by producing face masks had also occurred to a Congolese counterpart. In all likelihood, this counterpart was also a former rebel leader or retired general. He too probably owned a textile factory, manned by a single imprisoned employee. In any case, a lorry full of masks had arrived at the border. The sales team were older and more persistent than Riyyak's street-peddlers. They scattered themselves amongst the frightened fugitives, who had rejected point-blank Jamadi's idea of fighting fear with art, and instead opted for the age-old approach to killing time, that of Byzantine debate: which came first, the chicken or the egg? Jamadi had eventually joined in with the debate, taking the side of those who held that the chicken had come first. On several occasions, he had grown quite irate when justifying his stance.

The Congolese hawkers spread through the crowds with a speed comparable to Ebola itself. Theirs was a hard sell approach. Not a single person left maskless, except for the soldiers, who all bluntly refused to take one, since their orders made no mention of masks.

Another new development at the borders was the blossoming of a number of impulsive romances. Despite the climate of terror, many of the unmarried girls had found the borders to be the ideal setting for a little love affair, free from the obligations of letter-writing and the hopes and fears of marriage proposals. A touch of innocent excitement to invigorate their wait, and ensure they did not die before experiencing all the passion, anguish and pitfalls of love, as recounted since the dawn of time. The search for the handsomest, most chivalrous gentleman began in earnest. Needless to say, not a single glance was cast in Jamadi's direction.

Back in Nzara, Darina was not well. Just a year ago she had finally overcome her adolescent acne after numerous trips to various dermatologists, but now the spots had returned to plague her. Her sneezes had grown so intense that they made her knees tremble, and her itchy skin was driving her crazy, as if it was covered in insect bites and scabs. She had plainly heard on the organisers' radio that the first signs of infection were sneezing and joint pains, followed by bleeding. The sneezes were certainly there, and the joints of her hands were aching. Then she looked down and saw that her thighs were bleeding. Several times she stood up from her corner and promptly sat down again, looking over at Ruwadi, whose head was nodding as he dreamt of the beautiful women of Brussels. Of course he had never actually seen them, but had pieced their image together thanks to his particular ability to assemble disparate details into a complete picture.

Darina sensed the end was nigh: her very own finale. She only wished the virus would spare her long enough for her to find out whether the tennis player had really loved her and intended to marry her. For him, their meeting in the restaurant was simply a brief encounter, but for Darina, who had dwelled on the memory ever since, it was much more than that. Darina the human walking stick; at times, she so needed to rebel against that status, which was all she'd ever known.

Darina needed something to occupy herself with before the virus took hold fully, but there was no fruit to peel, and her hands were shaking too much to plait her hair. She could perhaps make some soft boiled eggs. There were eggs in the fancy kitchen, but she wasn't really hungry. This time, it was her who would bother Ruwadi, rousing him from his crowd of Belgian women. She would be the one attempting to beguile him with some funny language, for no reason other than to fight fear with trivialities.

'Ruwadi!' she called.

'Wait a minute, Darina,' came the musician's reply from the midst of his rosy dream, this one involving the most beautiful opera singer, a pure figment of his imagination whose sole job was to be star-struck by his fabulous performances. He was walking down the Galeries Royales with her in that very moment. He couldn't see her, of course, but he could feel her presence acutely.

'Hang on a minute, Darina – just until Maria Duncan has succeeded in sweeping me off to her hotel.'

Darina knew her companion's dreams well – those deep-rooted daydreams which followed him into sleep and made it very difficult for him to be roused. Ruwadi would concoct such fantasies when reality seemed so poisonous that there was no other way to carry on living. Those periods when days on end would pass without anyone inviting him to play a gig, or he wasn't in the right frame of mind to write a new song. Or when there was an unexpected coup in the country and his rivals – in an attempt to win over the new authorities – tried to align him with the old regime, which had summoned him dozens of times, demanding he obey their specific instructions to write something that would bolster their glory. In times such as these, Ruwadi would take refuge in his dreams, where he would abide for quite some time.

The dream came smoothly to an end. Maria Duncan took him back to the hotel and they kissed.

'Yes Darina? Is it over yet? Has Ebola stopped killing people? Can we go home now?'

'No,' came the girl's reply, standing so close it seemed she was about to kiss him, or provoke him into noticing her feminine qualities, which Ruwadi knew well. After all, he was the one who had raised her and sensed her grow from an innocent child into an attractive young woman.

Meanwhile, the francophones had moved to several rooms in the empty house, to calculate their losses, or await death. There they were, having left their homes and given themselves over completely to fear and anxious reflection. They had travelled far away from their families to take care of this star who, although he would probably never shine again even if the epidemic did pass, was in their care. It was their responsibility to look after him, whatever happened.

'Here's a random question for you,' Darina began, 'why have you never tried to grope me the whole time I've been with you?'

There was actually nothing arbitrary about the question at all. Darina was fighting her fear with a little lighthearted teasing – Ruwadi's response was a cruel blow announcing his decision to fight her teasing with pure heartlessness.

'Because you're too insignificant to deserve being groped by a star such as Ruwadi Monti. Get out of my face, Darina,' Ruwadi replied, having lost his temper completely. Despite his best efforts to justify the girl's behaviour – with reasons such as the state of terror they had both found themselves in – his anger was so overwhelming he could no longer control a single facial muscle.

Luckily for her, Darina escaped death at Ruwadi's angry hands thanks to a loud knock at the door. One of the concert organisers went running out from his room, adjusting his mask along the way. He was gone for some time before returning, shouting excitedly.

'Hey Ruwadi! Darina! Guys! It's time to party! We're saved! There are helicopters over Nzara – we're saved!'

The rest of the organisers came running half naked from their rooms, having attempted to strip themselves of their mental anxieties by removing their clothing. They ran out into the street, with Darina following.

'Hey guys! Hey Darina! What's going on?' Ruwadi called, having been abandoned.

FIFTEEN

'All hope is lost.'

To the ears of the overly optimistic, these are harsh words indeed; the cruellest and most soul-destroying of expressions.

Such words have been spoken throughout civilisation, handed down in memoire and oral narrative, sometimes fittingly, other times less so.

During a period of drought, a villager will shout that all hope is lost as a heavy cloud drifts by. All over the world, people declare their hopes in their elected ministers destroyed as the government turns sour. In many a lover's heart, all hope is abandoned as the moon that reminded them of their loved one fades from sight. Some lose their hope in Sudan – the world's grain-store – when they find its fields empty, others declare themselves disappointed by Gabriel Garcia Marquez's *Memories of My Melancholy Whores*. And perhaps somewhere, in an underground bunker where government rebels are bombarded, someone will declare, 'I lost all hope after that cockroach of a man died before I could gouge out his eyes and extract his fingernails.'

There are many such cases of disillusion, some world-famous: unrequited love, tragic death, sickness and dejection in all forms. Even the Mogul conqueror Genghis Khan had his disappointments, Alexander the Great too. One of the most famous phrases in history – 'And you, Brutus' – was, after all, the result of the complete loss of hope.

The despair felt by the refugees at the Congo-Sudan border, and the residents still cooped up in Nzara, was another to be added to this great catalogue. Their hope had been immense, circulating in whispered rumours of an impending aerial rescue mission.

In truth, nobody had known what the aircrafts would be carrying – medicine, equipment, high-tech masks, or purified air to be pumped into the atmosphere – nor had there been much effort to find out. After all, in circumstances such as these, the mere word 'rescue' in itself was more than enough.

At the border, where fear was now incarnate, crouching alongside each individual, the greatly anticipated helicopter fleet was spotted in the distance.

'Didn't I tell you!' screamed Jamadi Ahmed at the top of his voice.

As it happened, Jamadi hadn't mentioned a single word about a potential rescue mission. Such a wild idea hadn't occurred to anyone, and Jamadi in particular had been busy with his campaign of fighting Ebola with art, until his birds and rabbit had managed to escape through a hole in his bag. With the spectacular failure of his plans, Jamadi had joined the mass panic, immersing himself in the circuitous debate of the chicken and the egg.

'Didn't I tell you!' Jamadi cried again.

'What did you tell me?' asked his former admirer, who

had recently taken to ignoring him completely, her gaze fixed on the dark formations in the sky.

Jamadi couldn't remember what he had said, because he had never actually said anything. It was a fellow fugitive who had first put forward the notion of rescue.

'We're saved! They're here! We're saved!' cried the people, once the helicopters had drawn close enough for even their markings to be made out clearly. The aircrafts flew smoothly over the crowd and off into the distance. In their wake they left an immense and terrible despair; a loss of hope easily worthy of the history books.

The border guards had received no word of a rescue mission in the instructions that reached them continually both through the radio and in Morse code. They could not understand the mentality of the people swarming around them, since understanding was not in their instructions either. Pausing for breath between one philosophical conundrum and another, Jamadi tried accosting the same silver-bearded soldier who had previously told him of their egalitarian power structure. This time, Jamadi enquired as to whether there might be one humane instruction among their many orders – even an outdated order that was no longer applied – that would allow him to relocate women, children and the elderly, of which he was one. Jamadi informed the soldier that the people were in need of shelter and should not be left to languish outside for any longer. The soldiers should provide tents or permit them to use one of the large barracks where they could be terrified and desperate in some level of comfort.

The soldier was quite taken aback. Staring resolutely at a passing cloud, he towered over Jamadi as he spoke, reminding the musician once again of his own shamefully diminutive stature.

'Retreat civilian, retreat.'

The old magician stepped back, since there was nothing else he could do. At least it wouldn't be his preference for the egg over the chicken that would kill him. Indeed it was now looking rather plausible that an angry bullet might strike Jamadi down even before the virus could.

Back at Riyyak's factory – which, in line with the current trend, had changed its name from 'Jewel of the South' to 'Ebola Textiles' – Lewis Nawa continued to work the jobs of ten men, wolfing down egg and onion sandwiches and a porridge of vitrite tablets and millet Riyyak concocted himself. He even had a makeshift toilet Riyyak had dug out for him beneath the machine. That way, he didn't need to get up to answer the call of his terribly loose bowels. Hearing the thunder of an approaching fleet, Lewis gave a silent shout of joy to himself: 'I'm saved!' Riyyak approached the factory door with his machine gun on his shoulder, dressed from head to toe in camouflage. He opened the door cautiously and took a swift expert look at the sky.

'It's not one of our aircrafts, it's something else. Get back to work, Nawa.'

And Lewis did just that. Even having his hopes so thoroughly dashed had no effect on the cotton shirt he was weaving. Despair was impotent in the face of the unlicensed machine gun pointing his way, held by a rebel leader and potential dictator.

In Ebola Square, the sick were the only ones not to feel an overwhelming sense of despair as they sprawled beneath their damp rags, receiving liquid directly into their mouths now that the IVs had run dry.

It was the healthy, working away in their Riyyak Masks, and those who had revived after a deathbed awakening, who had their hopes dashed. The latter were busy monitoring the intermittent deathbed awakenings in order to sort the authentic from the inauthentic. They had hoped this task would soon be over, signalling their own escape from the threat of a painful death hanging over them too. They were tired of hearing the same confessions, each one so ugly and repetitive: husbands betraying wives, wives betraying husbands, bullying bosses and vengeful employees. One of the brothel women who had witnessed the sins of a number of respected tribal leaders began describing her life in lurid detail. A sober old man admitted writing secret love poems about school girls then tearing them up to hide the evidence. An Arab trader with an honest reputation confessed to selling Maggi Chicken Stock disguised as posh sweets. Meanwhile, the healthy population were eagerly awaiting what they hoped would be the more sensational of awakenings, such as that of James Riyyak, or the administrative officer with the overblown title of 'mayor,' or any of the foreigners from the well-barricaded compound. Surely theirs would provide some scandal with a hint of sophistication to it?

Meanwhile, in his upmarket residence, Ruwadi Monti was tripping over the furniture, stirred into action by the recent news and mentally preparing himself for a speedy exit, convinced the impending rescue mission was intended for him alone. It seemed his despair was preordained, as Darina emerged from the street, crying miserably. The organisers returned too, looking dismayed as they announced that the rescue mission was not for Nzara, and that Ruwadi would have to wait to revive his celebrity status as the Needle.

'Listen!' shouted one of the tour organisers, who by that point felt it would not be amiss to whip off his leather belt and give the delusional star a good hiding, or to pick up a wooden chair and launch it at his head.

'Listen Ruwadi, for the thousandth time, you're suffering no more than the rest of us. Don't you understand?'

Darina, convinced the virus had got her, had started to come to terms with her imminent demise, demonstrating all the traditional stages of grief as outlined in medical textbooks, even though she had no knowledge of them: shock, denial, acceptance, and hope.

Darina still had hope, and would hold onto it eternally. It was this that would save her from the despair reigning over the rest of the city.

As became apparent, the aircrafts churning up the dust and drowning out all other sound had not come for the victims, their helpers, or anyone else on that patch of diseased and arid land. Instead, the helicopters landed with decorum in an expatriate's back garden, there on a so-called humanitarian mission to extricate all those far from their home country, the people who had never in any way been Ebola's victims. The intrepid explorers clambered on board, thinking how their little run-in with a Third World epidemic was all part of the adventure. Meanwhile, the pilots assured the politicians and tribal leaders who had rushed to the scene that they would return, bringing doctors, rescue-workers and cures for ischaemia.

And thus began a new round of hope. This time, people were far more reluctant to participate, fearing the disillusion that was sure to follow.

SIXTEEN

This was not the end of the story. It could, in fact, have ended in any number of ways.

It was quite possible that Ebola would have its fill, or be struck by a sudden crisis of conscience and release its suffering victims. It had shown mercy to some in the past, granting them a humiliating but inauthentic deathbed awakening, before delivering them back to their wretched lives. The people were used to their miserable existence, and had been rather fond of it, before that unwelcome visitor had arrived in the libertine blood of a certain textile worker. Perhaps the misery of August would pass and by December the place would be clean again, despite the heat and humidity.

Perhaps the rescue team would return with the means to sanitise Ebola's breeding ground, forcing it to flee to some other location, or to revert to its state prior to that great outbreak, lying dormant in a Congolese village.

The fancy house where Ruwadi Monti and Darina were staying could well become their semi-permanent residence, where new and happy memories would be made. One of the francophone organisers might marry Darina in secret, so that she finally became mistress of a harmonious household. She would care for her family, whilst also continuing some of her former duties, nursing a sick old man who had once been something of a star, before begrudgingly fading away. Perhaps one of her children would smash his trusty guitar, or it would be soiled by a cat, or stolen, or simply lost in the general chaos of life, never to be rediscovered.

Perhaps Lewis Nawa would become living proof that continued application of pressure can only lead to explosion. He might return once more to the murderous fantasies that he had so often shooed from his mind – and perhaps this time he would be inspired to take advantage of a moment of sleep or absentmindedness on Riyyak's part and become his real-life assassin? The factory was deserted, and no one wanted to go near it. People would assume James Riyyak had fallen asleep with his machine gun in his lap, only to be peppered with bullets when the weapon went off accidentally. Thus would end the colourful life of a former rebel who, after throwing down his weapons and emerging from the jungle, had become a national treasure, an industrialist utterly loyal to his country. There would be no spectacular deathbed awakening, since a bullet leaves its target not even the time to scratch his nose or let out a final fart.

At the borders, perhaps nothing would change. Or a whole new city might spring up from nowhere – just a normal city called something or other, with streets and salesmen, parks and brothels, marriages, divorces, and love stories of every variety. There would be graves to bury the future dead in, and a street that looked just like Zumbi Street, turned by a bedazzled worker into Jamadi Ahmed Street, and owned by a decrepit magician no longer capable of performing his familiar tricks.